THE BARKS & BEANS CAFE
MYSTERY SERIES

FAIR TRADE

THE BARKS AND BEANS CAFE MYSTERY
SERIES: BOOK 3

HEATHER DAY GILBERT

Series: Gilbert, Heather Day. Barks & Beans Cafe Mystery; 3

Subject: Detective and Mystery Stories; Coffeehouses—Fiction; Dogs—Fiction
Genre: Mystery Fiction

Author Information & Newsletter: http://www.heatherdaygilbert.com

FROM THE BACK COVER

Welcome to the Barks & Beans Cafe, a quaint place where folks pet shelter dogs while enjoying a cup of java...and where murder sometimes pays a visit.

With the one-year anniversary of the now-successful Barks & Beans Cafe approaching, siblings Macy and Bo Hatfield set up an iced coffee booth at the state fair. Taking a break from brewing, Macy bumps into Carolina, a long-lost childhood friend who's now sitting pretty as a country superstar. Macy tries not to fangirl too hard when her old friend extends an invitation to meet the rest of the Carolina Crush band before their opening show.

But when Carolina falls victim to not one, but two near-death experiences, Macy takes it upon herself to find out who has it in for her old friend. Fortified with plenty of roasted corn, cinnamon rolls, and her brother's signature iced maple latte, Macy takes to the Ferris wheel to get the lay of the land from the air. She discovers too late that this year's fair isn't all fun and games...but she's already locked in for the ride.

Join siblings Macy and Bo Hatfield as they sniff out crimes in their hometown...with plenty of dogs along for the ride! The Barks & Beans Cafe cozy mystery series features a small town, an amateur sleuth, and no swearing or graphic scenes. Find all the books at heatherdaygilbert.com!

The Barks & Beans Cafe series in order:
Book 1: No Filter
Book 2: Iced Over
Book 3: Fair Trade
Book 4: Spilled Milk

1

"You forgot to tamp it again, Macy." My brother Bo sounded exasperated. "Remember how we practiced it?"

I sighed, hoping I wasn't all *that* bad. "How many iced lattes have I made today? And how many times did I forget to tamp before I pulled the espresso shots?"

Our Millennial barista Milo helpfully piped up. "I think you've tamped it a couple of times so far?"

We all knew I'd made at least twenty drinks today.

I shot him a glare, although it probably went unnoticed since my oversized shades had dark lenses.

In return, Milo gave me a grin. He sported brick-colored shorts, a polo shirt, Ray-Bans, and his dark blond hair was cut into a trim style that shouted high maintenance. He was a rich boy, and he didn't mind looking like one. He brought a certain moneyed vibe to the Barks & Beans Cafe that several of his wealthier Lewisburg friends seemed to appreciate. Especially those of the female variety, although I still suspected Milo was taken with our full-figured and big-hearted employee, Bristol.

Back in June, Bo had come up with the idea for setting up

an iced coffee stand at the West Virginia state fair this August, and I'd agreed it seemed an apropos way to expand our reach as we neared the one-year anniversary of the day we'd opened our dog-petting cafe. Together with our baristas, we'd brainstormed quite a few iced coffee and cold tea drinks that would be easy to replicate on the fairgrounds with limited equipment.

The only problem was, I was instructionally impaired when it came to making coffee. Up until now, I'd deliberately focused on building the Barks half of the cafe. We both knew I was the dog person, and Bo was the coffee person. But we didn't want to overwork our regular baristas in the August heat, so I'd volunteered to help with the booth as needed during the fair.

I was grateful I wasn't relegated to barista duties all day. Our friend Summer planned to bring a couple of shelter dogs over daily around lunchtime, allowing coffee customers to pet them in the shaded crate area. We wanted to continue our mission to match the shelter dogs to just the right humans, and there was no better place to have a little one-on-one contact than the fairgrounds. But the booth had been really busy this morning, so I'd had to up my coffee-brewing game in a relatively short amount of time.

Obviously, it had been too short, given my lack of tamping prowess. Bo had told me many times that if I didn't push the metal tamper down on the ground coffee before brewing it, the end result would be more water than coffee. No one wanted to pay for that.

I stepped aside as Bo took over to speed things up. Shooting an embarrassed glance toward the customers who were waiting at the front of the line, I met a pair of vivid blue eyes that looked a little desperate.

The dark-haired woman standing at the counter had ordered the iced raspberry latte I had attempted to make. A blond boy tugged at her arm, pointing at the kids' train ride across from us.

Next to her stood an older blonde woman holding a toddler girl with dark, curly hair and blue eyes exactly like younger woman's. I was guessing the blonde was the grandma.

The grandma leaned against the counter and gave it a quick rap with her red nails. "Hey there, hon, I'm not sure how long it's going to be, but we're sort of in a hurry. If you can't make me that frappe, we'll just grab Tess' iced latte and get outta your hair."

Bless his heart, Bo reached over and handed the older woman her caramel frappe. "I'm so sorry. We hadn't anticipated that opening day would be this busy."

The blonde woman gave an understanding nod and accepted her drink with a smile. Most women were easily charmed by my brother, who'd been blessed with red hair, muscles, and the kind of calm leader vibe that said everything was going to be okay.

The brunette leaned down to whisper something to the wiggly boy, then stood up, adjusting her purse. I didn't have to turn to know Bo and Milo were stealing glances at her. She was the kind of woman who stood out in a crowd, with her perfect-bow red lips and her incredibly porcelain skin. A study in contrasts, born to turn heads.

But her attitude was anything but diva. When her eyes met mine again, I felt the strangest sensation that we were kindred spirits. "It's fine. I think it's great what you're doing here—I read about your dog cafe online. We live up toward Ripley, but if we were closer, I'd visit Barks & Beans every chance I could. My husband Thomas is at a continuing education conference at the Greenbrier, and we thought it'd be a great chance for the kids to see the fair. But Mom and I are finding them a little hard to handle today."

The blonde took a sip of her drink. "It's the humidity. I'm guessing it's going to storm in a while."

I nodded. "I think so, too. I hope it'll stop before tomorrow night's opening show."

Everyone in the state knew about the fair's opening act, because it featured one of the highest-grossing country bands in existence—Carolina Crush. And the lead singer, Carolina Garten, had been born right in our hometown of Lewisburg, West Virginia.

In fact, Carolina had been my neighbor growing up.

I hoped I'd get a chance to see her, but I had decided against buying a ticket to either of her performances. They were pricey, and I'd recently started making car payments.

Milo handed the iced raspberry latte to the woman named Tess and she took a long, appreciative sip. "That's just what I needed—it's fantastic. Thank you all so much. Maybe we'll be back in your neck of the woods again someday and stop by the cafe."

I nodded, backing up so Milo could take the next person's order. I felt like a royal heel since I had no real barista skills. A strong arm draped over my shoulder and Bo raised an eyebrow.

"You really don't like making coffee, sis?"

"No, it's not that. It's just the pressure. I know you thrive under pressure, but I don't think I do. I make mistakes, especially when it involves multi-step processes like making coffee drinks."

He nodded, his bright blue eyes understanding. "You know what you need? A cinnamon roll break. Go over and get you one—and me, too, okay? Take an early lunch. I can handle the dogs when Summer brings them by...as long as you bring me a roll." He winked.

I heaved a sigh of relief. "Yeah, maybe I just need a little space. I hate to leave you and Milo alone, though—the line's getting bigger as we speak."

He walked back toward the counter. "If it gets to be too much, I'll call Kylie in."

Kylie was one of our other baristas, but she was supposed to have today off. I trudged away, mentally berating myself for not keeping my cool this morning.

The thing is, with dogs, you never have to worry about keeping your cool. You just notice them or pet them or play with them, and they'll always love you just the way you are. My Great Dane, Coal, was an excellent example of this. He loved me from the day he met me, and I knew he'd never stop loving me, no matter how many irritating or ill-informed things I did or said.

Making coffee was nothing like that. You either knew how to do it or you didn't, and I was starting to think I really didn't. Sure, I made my own drinks at home—London Fogs, strong French press coffee, chai lattes—but that wasn't the same as performing on demand for anxious and thirsty customers. Bo's coffee-making equipment was top-notch, and to be honest, the whirring grinder and whistling steam were only comforting to me when someone *else* was making coffee for the customers.

I found myself at the cinnamon roll booth, which was a tourist destination in and of itself. These guys knew how to run a business at the fair. They were fast and efficient, and I didn't see a frown on one customer's face.

Hopefully, Barks & Beans would eventually reach that status, but I was fairly certain that would require eliminating me as a barista.

I picked up the cinnamon rolls and stepped aside, watching teens as they screamed on the ride that lifted carts up on long arms and spun them around. It was called the Spider, and I'd always loved it. I determined to make time for a ride or two before the fair was over.

I used my hand sanitizer before grabbing a cinnamon roll. Once I sank my teeth into it, I let out a groan. Honestly, it was exactly what I'd needed.

A slim woman in a beat-up baseball cap chuckled nearby. "Good, isn't it? Those are the best."

I glanced at her, then did a double take. That long chestnut hair and the sprinkling of freckles across her entire face were all too familiar. Although her eyes were covered by aviator shades, I took a step closer. Dropping my voice, I murmured, "Carolina?"

The woman hesitated before pulling her sunglasses off. Wistful, pale blue eyes met mine and left no doubt. I was looking right at Carolina Garten herself.

Unceremoniously, I shoved my sunglasses up on my head. "Carolina! It's me, Macy Hatfield."

Now it was her turn to do a double take. She reached out to give me a hug, then pulled back to take another long look. "Good heavens, it *is* you! It's been so long. How old were we when I moved to Tennessee—eleven?" She gestured to my hair. "I'm so glad your color stayed just the same! I used to wonder why God didn't give me that perfect shade of marmalade he gave you."

I laughed. "If only you knew how many times I wished I could trade this marmalade mop for your smooth brown locks."

She clapped her hands, obviously excited. "I was going to pick up a roll, but I really want to catch up with you before I have to get back to the tour bus. Are you staying at your aunt Athaleen's place?"

I nodded. "Yes...actually, she passed away early last year."

Carolina teared up. "Oh, I hadn't heard! I'm so sorry. She was the sweetest. She made the best fresh-squeezed lemonade."

I closed my eyes, practically tasting Auntie A's sweet lemonade, which she'd always served with a fresh sprig of mint. I tried to stay chipper. "Actually, Bo and I have turned the front of her house into a cafe, and I live in the back half. It's called the Barks & Beans Cafe." I gestured to the left. "We're running a booth over that way, selling iced coffee drinks."

"Seriously? I've heard about that place—you can go in there and pet shelter dogs, right? You know I'm going to have to drop by soon." A cell phone pinged in her jeans pocket and she slid it out, reading a text on the screen. "Ugh. That's my manager, Murphy. I'd better grab my roll and get going. No rest for the weary and all that."

"I understand. I think it's great you're doing two concerts instead of just one. Very kind."

She gave a slight frown, grabbing both my arms. "Honestly, you were my best friend for so many years, Macy. I can't just leave you!" A smile slid across her lips. "Wait, I have a great idea. We're staying at the Greenbrier Resort, and they're serving us some kind of buffet meal in a private room tonight. You want to drop by and join us? I could introduce you to the band."

It was like she'd handed me the Golden Ticket to the chocolate factory. I'd never in my life have another opportunity to be so close to a group of famous people. My typical frozen lasagna supper paled in comparison to a private meal at the Greenbrier with Carolina Crush.

I grinned. "Just tell me the time and I'll be there."

As we exchanged phone numbers, I glanced up. A gaggle of teen girls was steadily edging closer to us, not-so-subtly snapping photos with their phones.

Apparently, I wasn't the only one who'd recognized Carolina.

I gave a nearly-imperceptible nod toward the girls and

Carolina got the message, sliding her aviators back on. "I'll text you," she whispered. She gave me a quick hug before striding directly into the path of heavy foot traffic, leaving the teens scrambling to track her down.

I was impressed. My awkward childhood friend had grown into a graceful, talented singer who was probably recognized nearly everywhere she went. I couldn't imagine what her life was like...but I was about to find out.

2

WHEN I DELIVERED the cinnamon roll to Bo and reported my run-in with Carolina, he gave a chuckle. "I still can't believe that gangly little girl next door turned into such a superstar."

"You didn't think she was a good friend for me." I knew my tone was sulky, but I didn't care. "I never understood why."

He shrugged, watching Milo as he prepared an iced mocha for a customer. Our customer line had petered out, but I knew when Summer arrived with the shelter dogs, things would pick up fast.

"I overheard Carolina saying something mean about Auntie A one time. I can't even remember what she said, but it was enough for me to write her off."

I elbowed him. "A little judgey, were you?"

He took another bite of cinnamon roll. "I guess so. I was used to you, and you weren't like that. You didn't talk behind people's backs."

I grinned at my brother's compliment. "Well, I'm not passing up this opportunity to meet the band just because you didn't like Carolina as a kid."

"I wouldn't expect you to," he said, finishing off his roll. "You go and have fun."

"What're you up to tonight?" I asked.

To my surprise, Bo blushed. "Uh—" His eyes trailed over to Summer, who was walking a couple of smaller dogs our way. "Here, let me help," he said, rushing over to open the crate for her.

"Thanks." Summer unleashed the dogs into the open-wire crate. Her honey-colored hair swung in a high ponytail and her brown eyes were fixed on my brother. He was standing awfully close to her, I noticed.

I had a flash of intuition. "So what's going on tonight, Bo?" I gave him a smug look, knowing I'd divined the source of his embarrassment.

Sure enough, his gaze traveled directly to Summer. "Uh, we're going out to eat."

"You're going on a date!" I practically shouted.

Summer laughed. "Don't get too excited or you might jinx it, Macy."

I immediately toned it down. I wanted nothing more than for my big brother to find happiness, and Summer was already one of my closest friends here. She was *so* much better for him than that controlling ex-fiancée of his, Tara.

"Y'all have fun." I daintily pulled my sunglasses down. "And I'll have fun at my band bash."

Summer's eyes widened. "Wait—are you talking about the band I think you're talking about?"

Bo nodded. "Oh, she is. She's proud of her secondhand fame, let me tell you." He walked over to help Milo.

Summer grabbed my arm. "Now it's your turn to tell me everything, Macy."

WHEN WE WERE SWITCHING shifts around two, I got a text from Carolina saying the dress for the private buffet was "smart casual."

It was too bad that Milo had already headed home, because he'd definitely know how to interpret the "smart casual" lingo for me. Jimmy had showed up for his shift, but he was older than I was and he always made it clear that he rarely dressed up for anything.

After chatting with Jimmy about his wife's flowerbeds and teasing Bo a little more about his upcoming date, I made my way across the fairgrounds to the parking area. I searched for my new white compact SUV, something I'd splurged on with my cafe income. It was my first brand-new car. I'd bought it because I could fold the back seat down and Coal could sprawl out, giving him far more room than he'd had in my old car, where he'd had to scrunch up to fit in front of the passenger seat.

It was a short drive to my house, which was right in town. Coal gave a few anxious whines as I unlocked my back door, and as soon as I opened it, he pounded past me to relieve himself in the fenced back garden.

"Well, hello to you too, you galloping brute." I turned to close the door, but Coal was already careening back toward me, bounding up the porch stairs in a single jump and skidding to a stop halfway through the door. Although he wasn't one of the more slobbery Danes, his jog had worked him up a little, so I grabbed a towel from the kitchen and wiped his jowls before he could shake his head and redistribute his spit to my walls.

"Tough day, huh?" I asked, heading over to refill his water bowl. He never seemed to get enough water, and would even wait until I refilled it before taking a bite of his food.

"I need to get ready for a smart casual buffet, Coal. What do you think about that?" He'd already started slurping at his water, so I dropped my keys and purse onto the counter and headed upstairs. After rummaging through my closet, I found a red Donna Karan twist-front dress I'd picked up from a consignment shop in South Carolina. It was a bright tomato shade that didn't clash with my hair. Unsure what shoes would work, I finally managed to dig up a pair of slightly beat-up black strappy heels that would have to do the job.

I sighed as Coal made his way into the room. "Sometime I need to invest in some new shoes."

He gave a short whining sound that broke into a yawn, as if he were agreeing with me.

"Right." I added another coat of mascara. "I mean, I'm glad Bo's dating, but I haven't gone out with anyone in months."

Again, Coal gave a yowl, which I felt was slightly accusatory.

"I know, I know. Dylan *has* asked me out. And I like him. It's just—" I glanced at my phone. "Oh, shoot, I need to move it." Unlike my brother, I had the tendency to arrive places just in the nick of time, if not a tad late.

After putting the finishing touches on my makeup, I turned on the TV for Coal and headed out. The sky had turned a leaden shade of gray, and it was obvious a thunderstorm was on the way.

By the time I got to the Greenbrier, thunder reverberated off the stone sidewalks and lightning arced through the sky. I barely managed to skitter into the large front doors and onto the green carpet before the rain picked up. I shook off my umbrella, hoping the humidity hadn't puffed my hair into a mushroom cloud.

The Greenbrier was a good-sized resort, and I had to walk quite a way to reach the private reception room. Before heading into the open double doors, I darted into one of the bathrooms

—which were as posh as small living rooms—and tried to tamp down my thick waves.

Feeling as ready as I'd ever be, I headed into the reception room. I glanced around and got the sinking feeling I was overdressed.

Men were sitting around in button-up shirts with no ties, and one woman wore a flowy pantsuit. Carolina herself wore black leather pants and a pinstriped, sleeveless blouse. Her hair was tossed artlessly into a bun and secured with black chopsticks. She hurried over the moment she saw me.

She gave me a concerned once-over, her cornflower-blue eyes looking catlike with her dark liner and shadow. "Macy! I'm so glad you made it. It's a wonder you weren't drenched! The rain was beating against those big windows and I was worried about you." She tucked an arm under my own and steered me toward the reception table. It had been beautifully laid out, complete with china dishes. The theme seemed to be Italian food, and everything looked delectable. I looked forward to feasting on the olive bread, Tuscan bean soup, and sausage-stuffed sweet peppers, among other things.

Carolina walked me back to her table. I recognized the dark-bearded man sitting next to her as Anthony "Tony" Garten, her husband. He wore round glasses with blue-tinted lenses. Nodding at me, he speared a meatball with his fork. "The food of my people," he said, feigning an Italian accent.

Across the table, a younger woman shot him a glare. "You're barely Italian at all."

His dark eyes narrowed. "So says the woman who plays on her minimal Spanish heritage in every blinking interview she does."

Carolina gave her husband a silencing look before turning to the woman. "Reya, this is my friend Macy. We were next door neighbors when we were kids. Macy, Reya Heres is my backup singer." She placed a hand on the dark-bearded man's shoulder. "And you've probably guessed this is my husband, Tony."

Reya, whose platinum hair sported dark brown roots, met my eyes and managed a brief, tight smile. Tony must've been getting on her nerves for some time, because she quickly turned her back to us, striking up a conversation with an older, balding man who was carefully attempting to set his heaped-full plate on the table.

As I sipped at my soup, Carolina introduced me to the moody-looking man sitting opposite her, but I already knew his name. Gage Hansen was not only the guitarist for the band, but he was also the lead male vocalist. In contrast, Tony was always in the background on the piano or dulcimer, which gave the band its unique sound. I often wondered if Gage's frontman status made Tony jealous, but that was probably because the tabloids loved speculating to that effect.

Gage was in his late twenties, with longer, dirty blond hair and noticeably angular cheekbones. He looked more rock-n-roll than country in his casual T-shirt and hoodie. He must not have received the "smart casual" memo.

His piercing green eyes focused on me. Unsettled by his scrutiny, I ducked down, fumbling for my fork.

Carolina noticed my unease and dropped her voice. "You okay?"

I took a bite of salad, waiting for Gage's attention to shift elsewhere before answering. "Yeah. He just reminded me a little of my ex. He had green eyes like that."

Carolina dug into her tiramisu. "Wow, I didn't even realize you'd been married. I hate that we fell so out of touch."

The balding man, whose accent sounded a little New Jersey, said, "So, Carolina, are you going to introduce me to your lovely friend?"

Carolina dabbed at her lips with a napkin, leaving behind a smear of light pink gloss. "I'm sorry, but you were busy talking. Murphy, this is Macy Hatfield, my childhood friend. And Macy, this is Murphy Peters, my manager."

The man gave me a warm smile. "You must be a special friend—Carolina rarely takes anyone behind the scenes, as it were. Have you showed her around the tour bus, Caro?"

Carolina cringed, and I knew why. She'd always hated that nickname and had once slugged a kid in second grade for calling her that. I'd never figured out why it was so abominable to her, but I'd guessed that it reminded her of Karo syrup, something Auntie A always kept on hand in case we got "a touch constipated."

"I haven't, but I will soon." She wrapped an arm around my shoulder. "Macy here runs a dog cafe called Barks & Beans. It's downtown." Her tone was proud, as if I were a regular superstar myself.

I blushed. "Well, my brother and I do. And it's sort of a dog-petting cafe. I mean, we don't bake dog treats or anything. In fact, we have an excellent baker who makes the most amazing sandwiches and desserts..." I knew I was rambling, but I didn't know how to stop.

Murphy's attention had already returned to his plate. "Mm-hm, is that so?" he murmured, spearing a piece of asparagus.

Gage leaned in, those unnerving eyes once again fixing on me. "I find that intensely interesting, Macy. What kinds of dogs do you have there?"

I forced myself to look at him. He was just a regular guy like anyone else. Just because he reminded me of Jake didn't mean he was automatically untrustworthy.

Warming to the topic, I explained that shelter dogs were rotated in daily for customers to pet while they sipped their coffee drinks, or if they preferred, they could stay in the

Beans section and simply watch the dogs frolic in the Barks section. "It's great to see a lot of these cast-off dogs form bonds with customers, and we have a really high adoption rate."

Gage's rapt attention seemed to wane. I had a strong suspicion he wasn't the dog-adopting type. "That's great," he said. He stood, pushing his chair in. "Excuse me while I get some dessert. Would you like anything, Macy?"

I wasn't even finished with the main course. "No, thanks."

As he walked away, Carolina yawned. "I'm sorry—I'm still kind of exhausted from riding in the Crush Bus yesterday—that's what we call our tour bus. Would you mind if I call it a night?"

While I hadn't anticipated my hostess abandoning me, I understood. "Oh, sure. You need to be in tip-top shape for the opening performance tomorrow night. I know everyone is looking forward to it."

"Are you coming?"

I felt sheepish. "By the time I thought to check, the tickets were nearly sold out and so expensive. I figured I'd be tired out from working the coffee booth—"

Carolina held up a slim hand, stopping me. "I absolutely won't hear of you missing it! I want you and Bo to come—tickets are on me." She interrupted Murphy, who'd fallen back into conversation with Reya. "Murph, can you get me two tickets for tomorrow? Good ones, I mean?"

The man nodded. "Of course. We always save a few seats for VIPs."

Carolina chuckled and nudged me. "You and Bo can be my VIPs."

I thanked her before she grabbed her black leather clutch and strode purposefully out of the reception room. It struck me as odd that she didn't even say any goodbyes, but she *was* the lead singer, and she certainly didn't have to answer to anyone. Plus, she saw these people every day.

As I hurried to polish off the rest of my stuffed pepper, I stole glances at the other band members. Tony seemed a little uncouth—he was picking something out of his teeth with his fork. Reya was gesturing forcefully to Murphy, perhaps trying to prove some kind of point. Gage wiped his mouth before motioning to Tony. The two men seemed to have an understanding, because they both stood up and placed their napkins on the table.

"We're heading down to the casino," Gage announced to the table at large.

Murphy's eyebrows inched up, but he simply nodded.

"See ya." Reya sounded dismissive. She adjusted her pink blouse and picked up her discussion with Murphy.

Since no one was making an effort to talk with me, I figured my dinner had come to an end. Although the artfully-designed chocolate tart was calling my name, I preferred to satisfy my sweet tooth at home with a s'more. I still had a few chocolate bars leftover from our last bonfire in Bo's back yard.

I arranged my used fork and knife across my plate. Leaning in toward Murphy and Reya, I said, "Thanks for letting me drop by."

Murphy gave me an absent nod, and Reya forced a half-smile. "Sure, anytime," she said.

Feeling like a complete third wheel, I leaned down to gather my umbrella and purse. As I strode out, my heels left tiny impressions in the plush carpeting.

I couldn't help mulling things over as I made my way downstairs. The private buffet had left a sour taste in my mouth. But why? Was I jealous of the lives of the rich and famous?

I didn't think that was it. Bo and I had several wealthy

friends, and my brother was far from a pauper himself, given his early retirement as vice president of the coffee bean distributor Coffee Mass. His coffee job had also been a front for his DEA work, so he'd had that stream of income, too.

Of course, I hadn't made out quite as well when I left the DMV after Jake divorced me. Maybe I was feeling a little raw that Jake was now spending his substantial car dealership income on a new honey? I shook my head. It had never been about money when I married Jake. I had been powerless to fight my attraction to him, plain and simple.

Since our divorce, I'd had plenty of time to kick myself that I'd ignored my gut instincts when we were dating. Jake was always hyper-aware of his good looks, and I'd later discovered that he wasn't above using them to get whatever he wanted.

I stumbled off the elevator. The casino sounded like it was in full swing. Maybe that's what was niggling at me—the fact that Tony would only head to the casino *after* his wife left the room. Was he a secret gambler? Or had Jake's cheating made me distrust the motivations of husbands in general?

I pushed the front door open, thankful to see the rain had stopped. After walking the long distance to my car, I sank into the driver's seat. Of course I was happy for Carolina's success, but something seemed to be amiss with the Carolina Crush group dynamics. It would be interesting to see how the band pulled together on the stage tomorrow night.

Once I got home, I hadn't even pulled my shoes off before Coal plastered his long body against my legs. I stroked his ears. "I love you, too, but I need to move. How about you go potty?" I pushed the door open and he lumbered out.

I was just cracking open a fresh water bottle when Carolina called, her voice croaky. "Macy? You're not going to believe this, but I'm in the hospital."

3

I STOOD for a moment in stunned silence. "Wait. What's happened?" My mind raced through all kinds of scenarios. "Is Tony there with you?"

She gave a small groan. "Not yet. The doctors are keeping me isolated for now. It's the weirdest thing." When she hesitated, I heard people bustling around her. "I'd just gotten back to my room when I started having these awful stomach cramps. I brushed it off at first, but by the time I got in the shower, I was doubled over, vomiting my guts out. I managed to call for help before I passed out."

"Good grief! Are you okay? What is it, a stomach bug? Food poisoning?" Either option could mean I was next in line for this illness. I certainly hadn't been stingy with my portions at dinner.

"They're not sure." She gave a dry cough. "They're running some tests. I just wanted to let you know that they had to cancel tomorrow night's show. But don't worry—I'll have your tickets bumped to the Saturday night performance. I should be better by then."

I clicked my tongue. "I don't know if you'd better perform at all. What're the doctors saying?"

"Well, I just got moved into a room, so I haven't talked to one since the ER doc admitted me. I'll let you know as soon as I hear something definite."

Coal lightly bopped his front paw into the screen door, so I opened the door to let him in. He pranced directly over to his water dish and sat down next to it, waiting for a refill.

"Did you need me to call anyone for you?" I asked Carolina. I was still unclear as to whether she had let anyone else know what was going on. For all I knew, Tony and Gage could still be living it up in the casino.

She made a gagging sound. "Gotta go. I'm not feeling right. I —told Murphy." She abruptly hung up.

I hoped she was able to press the call button. Most people wouldn't be hospitalized for a stomach bug, but since Carolina was who she was, she probably had certain privileges. Maybe even a private room. And I was glad, because she didn't really seem to have a strong support system. Apparently, Tony wasn't the first in line to be informed in times of distress. Instead, Carolina's manager was.

I wanted to call Bo and let him know what had transpired this evening, but he was probably still out on his date. The thought made me grin as I poured water into Coal's bowl. Summer was very different from the rather imperious women Bo had dated in the past—especially Tara, the one he'd asked to marry him last year. Tara wound up breaking the engagement, choosing to believe lies about my brother. I knew it had done a number on his confidence, which is likely why it had taken so long for him to gather his courage to ask Summer out.

Sure, Summer was driven in her own ways. Her life largely revolved around running the animal shelter and finding homes for the pets. Just this year, she'd instituted a pet fostering program that had really taken off. But she was never bossy or demanding in how she related to people. Maybe it was her Mennonite upbringing, but she oozed humility in everything she did. That was definitely part of why I liked her so much.

She was perfect for Bo, but we'd have to wait until he saw that for himself.

I headed upstairs to change, Coal at my heels. He didn't like to be far from me at any given time. "I'm coming right back," I explained to him. "You go sit on the couch."

His ears, which always stood up because they'd been cropped by his previous owner, did a little back twist when he recognized the word "couch." It was a treat for him to sit there, so he hurried over to climb into his favorite spot.

Upstairs, I rummaged in my dresser drawers and found my comfy yoga pants and a tank top. After putting those on, I grabbed a hair elastic and pulled my voluminous mane into a bun. If I had to start puking, I wanted to be ready.

Hopefully, Carolina was feeling much better. It seemed odd that she'd fallen so violently ill and I wasn't. Stomach bugs usually moved quicker than that.

And if it were food poisoning, I should also be sick. Carolina had recommended the soup and the stuffed pepper, so I'd assumed she'd eaten the same things before I arrived.

If I had Murphy's number, I could call and ask if anyone else at the meal was suffering from food poisoning. To avoid calling Carolina, I decided to try my luck and asked the Greenbrier to put me through to him.

Unfortunately, they wouldn't, but they did take a message with my cell number. I headed downstairs and set the pot on to boil for some peppermint tea, hoping it would deter any impending stomach issues.

Coal's sprawling body took up two seats' worth of space on the couch, leaving one cushion for me. I sighed, noting the ever-expanding worn patches on the fabric. I was going to have to invest in a more durable couch—maybe leather? Something that could stand up to Coal's heavy body shifting around on it.

I turned on the TV and was flipping through shows when my phone rang. Hoping the unrecognizable number was Murphy, I picked up.

Sure enough, a New Jersey accent filled the line. "Hi, Macy. They told me you'd called. I take it Carolina has been in touch with you?"

"She called. Is she any better? Also, I was wondering if anyone else had gotten sick?"

I heard a woman speaking in the background, and Murphy sounded distracted when he responded. "She's not recovering as quickly as I would hope. In fact, I'm trying to come up with a backup plan for the concert Saturday." His voice got muffled and he barked out, "Get another outfit—you look like a druggie."

I wondered if he were talking with Reya, although she'd seemed well dressed when I met her.

As he returned to the phone, he apologized. "Sorry. We're in the Crush Bus trying to run through things, and Gage seems to have misunderstood what country singers are supposed to look like."

I could tell that Murphy wanted to get off the phone, but I wasn't ready to let him go. "Does Tony know what's going on with his wife? Is anyone else sick?"

"What? Oh, yeah, Tony knows. He's here, too, helping me figure out songs they can do without Carolina. And no one else is sick."

I was stumped. "Do the doctors think it's food poisoning rather than a stomach bug?"

Murphy huffed. "I have no idea. To be honest, your hick hospital isn't doing a great job of staying in touch with me about my client. If she were in Nashville—"

I'd heard enough. No one insulted my town. "Maybe you'll hear from them soon. I'll let you go for now." I hung up.

I sank into the couch, stroking Coal's silky head. The silent red flags I'd picked up on earlier were now whipping in the wind, practically shouting for attention. If Carolina had a stomach bug or food poisoning, it seemed logical that at least one other person would be throwing up by now.

Instead, no one else was sick, and that made me very nervous. Add to that the fact that Murphy was moving forward with Saturday concert plans...which probably meant he was conveniently shifting Reya to the forefront as lead singer, in case Carolina felt too bad to perform.

I took a sip of peppermint tea. Given the tense dynamics at the meal tonight, I couldn't shake the feeling that something more than a fluke stomach bug was at play. She was down for the count at a critical juncture, right before the first fair concert. Could it be possible that someone wanted her out of the picture—at least for a while—and was unscrupulous enough to poison her?

It was worth looking into. I picked up my phone and called one of Auntie A's closest friends—our family practice doctor from childhood. Doctor Stan Stokes had seen just about every ailment out there. He'd been the first to suggest that Auntie A might have cancer, although by that time it had unfortunately progressed too far. He would know if something was wonky in Carolina's case. He was retired, but he still made regular rounds at the hospital, so he might overhear things or even drop in on her.

He greeted me warmly when he picked up the phone. "Macy Hatfield. What a delight to hear from you. I still recall that time you nearly had me convinced there'd been a mistake and that Bo was there for his school shots instead of you."

The man never tired of telling that story. My tremendous

fib had been born out of desperation—I had a phobia of shots. Still did, in fact. "Yes, I remember. Auntie A didn't take long to put that lie right, though. We made a swift trip to the bathroom and she made sure I got my story straight."

He chuckled. "Not the best way to kick off your office visit, I'm afraid. Now, what can I help you with?"

I explained the situation with Carolina. "Am I overly suspicious to wonder if she's been poisoned?" I asked.

He didn't hesitate. "Given what you've told me, I think there's legitimate cause for concern. I'll find out who her doctor is and suggest he check things out if he hasn't already." His voice lowered. "If it is poisoning, there can be long-term damage to the liver. It's imperative that she gets tested immediately."

I said a hurried goodbye so Doctor Stokes could get the ball rolling for Carolina. Coal was snoring lightly as I flipped to one of my favorite real estate shows and turned the volume up. An hour flew by, and when the show was winding up, Doctor Stokes called back.

"I can't say much since it's not my case, but let's just say you were on the right track," he told me. "You'll want to get the details from Carolina, but things were caught in time, so she should be on her way to recovery."

I pressed my hand to my chest, completely floored that my guess had been right. "She really dodged a bullet, then."

After saying goodbye to the doctor, I hesitated. Should I call Carolina, who was likely feeling completely wrung-out at this point? I decided against it. Doctor Stokes had assuaged my fears in large part by indicating that although Carolina was likely poisoned, she was also going to come out of it safely.

Had Murphy or Tony been informed of what had really happened to Carolina? I had to assume the doctor or the hospital would've updated them on her recovery, since they must be listed as her emergency contacts.

Deciding that there wasn't much more I could do, I settled back into the couch with Coal. My eyelids kept fluttering shut, so I finally turned off the TV, placed my mug in the sink, and let Coal out to use the bathroom. The relentless heat of the fairground and the stress of making coffee drinks had definitely zapped my energy. I wasn't looking forward to more of the same tomorrow, but I was excited about one thing...finding out how date night went for Bo and Summer.

4

BRISTOL WAS the first to show up at our booth in the morning, which was unusual. Bo was always the first to arrive, often a full fifteen minutes early. I now understood that it was his DEA training that pushed him to map out a new area and know all the emergency exits, so he'd have an advantage over any ne'er-do-well who happened to appear.

Bristol's glossy dark hair brushed her waist as she bustled around, setting up the creamer and sugar packets. I was amazed at how quickly her hair had grown just over the summer. Her bubblegum pink nails matched her lips. She wasn't afraid to be bold with her clothing and accessory choices, and she had a flair for design. Although she was amazing with the shelter dogs and had quickly become my right-hand woman in the Barks section of the cafe, she'd recently determined to go to college and get the graphic design degree she'd always longed for. Although her single mom couldn't contribute much to her continuing education, Bristol hoped to have enough saved up by next fall to attend college.

Bo and I were already plotting to make anonymous yearly

donations to Bristol's college fund. If anyone deserved a chance to succeed, it was Bristol Goddard.

She sank into a crouch, trying to retrieve something behind the counter. "Where's Mr. Hatfield?"

Although we did encourage our employees to call us *Mister* and *Miss Hatfield*, to keep it clear we were the owners, the words always sounded especially respectful coming out of Bristol's mouth.

"I'm not sure—"

Someone grabbed me from behind in a bear hug and swung me around. Before I could stop to process things, I let out a loud squeal.

Bo gave a chuckle, setting me back on the ground. "Talking about me behind my back, are you?"

Bristol giggled as she rose to her feet. "No, sir. We just wondered where you were."

Recovering my dignity, I put my hands on my hips and squared off toward Bo. "Thanks," I said sarcastically. "I sure needed a shot of adrenaline this early in the morning. Anyway, why did you show up late, pray tell? Could it have anything to do with your *date?*"

Bo seemed to take my meddlesome question seriously. "No, we went home around ten, so we weren't out too late. I just took a little longer in the shower, that's all." He rubbed at his chin...which I suddenly realized was clean-shaven.

"You cut off your *beard!*" I shouted, kicking myself for not having a better eye for details. I had to believe most women would've been quicker to notice if their brother shaved off a beard he'd worn for years. "But what will Summer think?"

He widened his stance. "Do you really think Summer's so attached to the beard? It was just getting a little long, and I didn't want to mess with trimming it."

Bristol pulled her cat-eye sunglasses down for a better look.

"It looks good," she declared. She pushed her shades back up, because the sun was already blazing.

I had to reserve judgment since I was so used to seeing Bo with a beard. Plus, Charity had arrived to deliver our wrapped bakery items for the day, and the cheesecake Danish was calling my name.

"We'll talk more later." I gave Charity a hug and snatched a Danish. As I peeled the plastic wrap from it, the scent of pure buttery goodness hit me. "Charity," I said, "I love all your new recipes, but old standbys like this one always make my day."

Charity gave an understanding nod of her snowy-white head. She had a youthful, cherubic face, which served her well since she was raising her five-year-old grandson entirely on her own. "I'm working on revamping some of the cafe favorites for fall. Think pumpkin, caramel, and cinnamon."

"Mm," Bristol said.

I left the two women to talk and walked over to Bo. In a low tone, I filled him in on all the events of last evening, including Carolina's poisoning.

It was hard to shock my brother, but I could tell he was surprised. "Who would hate Carolina enough to poison her?" he asked. "I would imagine she's the driving reason for the band's success—I mean, after all, it's called *Carolina Crush*."

"Right." I toyed with motives that would push someone to poison Carolina. "Let's say Reya Heres wanted a chance to be lead singer. Well, a state fair is a big venue, isn't it? Maybe she just meant to sideline Carolina, not kill her."

He pulled out a bag of our house blend coffee and opened it. The strong scent of the Costa Rican beans hit me square on, waking me up a little. "Sure, that's possible, especially if the manager is going to move her to lead singer tomorrow night," he said.

"I think he will, unless Carolina feels a lot better. She sounded miserable."

"It would really depend on how much poison they gave her —if they even did. That sounds like something the police should be looking into. Do you think Detective Hatcher's been pulled in on this?"

Detective Charlie Hatcher had worked with us before, and he was never stingy with his information, since Bo was ex-DEA. Sometimes I got the feeling he wished Bo would forget the cafe and join him as a detective.

"I'm not sure. I figure they're keeping things hush-hush for now."

"Attempted poisoning is not something you can hush up," Bo said grimly. "I'll check with the detective."

"Thanks." A line had formed at our booth, so we needed to get busy helping Bristol and Charity. "I'm going to call Carolina on lunch break and see how she's doing."

"Sounds good. Let me know." Bo dumped beans in the grinder. "And sis...just be careful around the band. They live in a whole different world."

"Not Carolina," I said. "She grew up right next door."

SUMMER STOPPED in around lunch and introduced me to the dogs she was dropping off today. After listening with only half an ear to her descriptions of the friendly pups, I brought the conversation around to the more pressing topic of how she enjoyed her date with Bo.

Her dark eyes crinkled at the corners as she smiled. "We went to that fusion restaurant you'd recommended. Say, didn't you go there with *Dylan?*" she teased.

I gave a brief nod. "Don't try to distract me. And what did you eat?"

"Bo got the chicken curry and I had some kind of French duck dish—"

"Duck confit shepherd's pie," Bo interrupted, adding whipped cream to the top of an iced drink.

Summer nodded. "I got it because I thought the pie looked amazing, but I have to admit, the duck wasn't my favorite."

I took Summer's arm and led her away from Bo. "Did you have a good time?"

"I did," she said. She was practically glowing. "Your brother is a special man. I had fun getting to know him."

"And you think he looks okay without the beard?" I pressed.

Summer looked at Bo, her eyes lingering. She gave a shy laugh. "I sure do."

I let go of her arm with a contented sigh. "I'm so pleased that everything went every bit as great as I'd hoped."

Summer gave me a quick hug. "Thank you for talking me up to Bo."

I shook my head. "Nonsense. You require no 'talking up,' my friend. Now, if you'll excuse me, I need to make a call."

Summer walked over to Bo and I plopped into the folding chair near the dog crate to make my call. Carolina picked up on the first ring.

"I'm so glad you called. I'm losing my mind in here. I need to be at the rehearsal for tomorrow night's show." Her voice seemed to have returned to normal.

"Hold up there," I said. "What did the doctor say about the show? Or about how soon you'll be out?"

Determination charged her words. "He didn't say, but Murphy's coming over to get me out of here."

I pushed my bangs off my hot forehead. "You need to take it easy. Did the doctor tell you what had happened?"

"I overheard Doctor Stokes talking to my doctor in the hallway. He said you'd suggested checking for poison in my system?"

"Yes, I did. It didn't make sense that you had food poisoning or a stomach bug, since no one else got sick."

She gave a light groan. "Well, it turns out you were right. As soon as my doctor got the tests back, he gave me activated charcoal and some other medicine. They were able to stop things before any permanent damage was done. Thanks for giving him a heads-up."

I smiled at a couple of children who were standing by their parents in the coffee line. I had a feeling that Charity's brightly colored cake pops were going to be a hot item today—that, or the coffee-free cream frappe drink. Next year, we planned to invent more kid-friendly iced drinks. We'd considered selling lemonade, but since there were always a couple of fresh-squeezed lemonade stands on the fairgrounds, we'd decided against it.

"Carolina, you can't just blow this whole thing off and rush back into performing. The issue here is that someone—maybe even one of your band members—just poisoned you. It's reasonable to assume that someone wants you dead, and they might try again since they were unsuccessful."

Carolina probably wasn't used to getting scolded by her peers, and she sounded touchy. "I'm not going to let them. Listen, I'm going to have the hotel staff bring meals directly to my room from now on. No more banquets for me. And once our shows are over, I might be making some big changes anyway." She sounded like she was struggling to sit up in bed. "I need to run. Murphy's here and he's talked to the doctor. I'll finish recuperating at the Greenbrier—*after* I rehearse for the concert."

I thought about voicing a final protest, but clearly Carolina wasn't listening to a word I said. "Okay, I guess I'll see you at the concert tomorrow, if not before."

I hung up, wishing Murphy would use his managerial influence to talk some sense into Carolina instead of springing her from the hospital. She couldn't be back up to par yet. But I supposed that like Bo said, Carolina was the real cash cow of the band. She was the one the crowds paid to see, and she was the one the media couldn't get enough of.

Had Murphy let the media know about Carolina's poisoning yet? I plugged her name into my phone's search bar and in less than a split-second, headlines popped up trumpeting her near-death experience in West Virginia. Apparently, Murphy hadn't hesitated to spill the beans about his client's close call. He was a regular mercenary, but I supposed most music managers were.

Maybe it was true that "any publicity was good publicity," but for my old friend's sake, I hoped she'd seen the beginning and end of her newsworthy close calls.

5

I STAYED busy as Friday seemed to rush by. Since a cool breeze had picked up, I'd decided the dogs could stay an extra hour. Quite a few customers lingered to pet them. In fact, one family fell in love with the peppy dog that looked like a smaller-sized Jack Russell terrier. They went directly to the animal shelter to fill out the paperwork.

I took a break to grab an easy supper for Bo and me—hot dogs with chili and coleslaw and a side of roasted corn. Bo and I sat down and ate our overpriced meal, which seemed to hit the spot. Bristol and Charity had already headed home, so we were on duty until closing.

"It's been a long couple of days," I admitted, taking a bite of corn. "I'm glad I'm back in the cafe tomorrow. I've been kind of jealous of the employees who've been there in the air conditioning." I looked over at my brother, who was wiping chili from his chin. "You sure you're up for working the booth tomorrow, too?"

He nodded, picking up his corn. He was one of those typewriter-style corn eaters—working his way along in neat rows. Meanwhile, I just took random bites until the whole cob was finished. I felt there was a metaphor in there somewhere—kind of like a corn-eating personality test. Salt or butter? Pepper? Eating in complete chaos or in an orderly fashion?

"Oh, yeah, I'm fine working out here." He grinned. "Sis, you *do* realize that I've been in much hotter places than West Virginia."

Someday I wanted to hear all about the countries Bo had traveled to when he was with the DEA—but not today. He still didn't have complete closure from that job, even though he'd retired from it. My brother had once gotten way too close to taking down a super-villain named Leo Moreau, and last year, Leo made it clear he still kept tabs on Bo...and even on me. It was unnerving, knowing a criminal mastermind might be watching you when you least expected it.

Not to mention, Moreau's conniving wife, Anne Louise, had reached out to my brother of her own accord. She had been friendly to him—which made his DEA and FBI friends worry even more. She hadn't contacted Bo since last winter, but she'd insinuated she needed to talk with him someday, so everyone was waiting to see when the penny would drop and she'd reach out to Bo again.

"I'm sure you have." I wiped butter from my mouth. "Hey, do you feel like an iced coffee?"

Bo heard the request in my question—he knew I didn't want to get up and make the drinks. "I'll fix us some. Does iced maple latte sound good?"

I smiled, thankful my brother could read me so well. "I'd love one."

ONCE WE'D CLOSED UP, I made a detour on the way to my car, hunting for the Crush Bus. I doubted that Carolina would be there, but if someone was, I thought they might let me take a little tour. I probably wouldn't get another chance to do it, once their performances were underway.

The bus was easy to spot—it was emblazoned with the band's distinctive coral-colored logo, along with "Crush Bus" written in bold cursive lettering. Lights were on inside, so I approached the door.

However, a large man in dress pants and a headset approached from the front of the bus, giving me a once-over. "Were they expecting you?"

I assumed he must be a bodyguard. "Yes—Murphy Peters and Carolina invited me to see inside the tour bus. I'm Macy Hatfield."

The man spoke into the microphone before giving me a brief nod. He rapped five times on the door, and Murphy opened it. He squinted into the dim twilight.

"Hi, Murphy. I'm Macy Hatfield—we met last night. You mentioned I should visit the tour bus sometime, and this will probably be my best chance. Unless that doesn't work for you?"

He gave me a wan smile. "A lot's happened since last night, hasn't it? Sure, come on into our Crush Bus. I'll take you back to see Caro in the music room."

It was good to hear that Carolina was out and about, but at the same time, I still felt she was pushing herself too hard.

Stepping into the bus, I gasped at the top-quality decor. A dark leather couch and chair lined one wall. At least twenty battery-operated candles glowed on a small granite side table. The wood flooring looked warm and inviting, and it was topped with several deep blue Persian rugs. Reya stepped out of the sleek kitchenette with a mug in her hands and nodded at me before dropping onto a couch.

"Is everyone here?" I asked, following Murphy as he made his way toward the opposite end of the bus.

"Just Reya, Gage, and Carolina, at the moment. Tony headed out early." Murphy pushed open a double door and I came to a full stop, staring at the fully-equipped music studio.

Gage and Carolina were sitting close together, watching a recorded band performance on the drop-down TV screen. After pausing the video, Carolina walked over to my side.

"Macy! I'm so glad you dropped in! How are things at your coffee booth?"

"Good—but I'm the one who should be asking how things are with *you*. Are you feeling any better?"

She nodded, dark hair swirling over her shoulders. "Definitely. I think that charcoal stuff did a total purge, you know? I should be out of the woods."

Murphy took a seat. "That's what your doctor said."

I glanced at the two men, unsure if this was a good place to talk about the poisoning. Carolina followed my gaze and seemed to realize that I wanted to chat. She placed a hand on my elbow. "Say, are you game for a ride on the Ferris wheel? I think I could squeeze in one go-round, and it would bring back old times. It's always so pretty at night."

I grabbed at the opportunity. "Sure. Let's go."

Carolina turned and said, "We'll be back soon, I promise. And Gage, go over that tape from the Georgia state fair—I think we need to position ourselves on this stage the same way we did there."

Gage gave a slow nod, his eyes still fixed to the screen. Murphy gave a grunt of approval and we hurried out.

As we walked past Reya, she turned her back on us to look at her phone. It didn't take any special insight to pick up on the tension in the air. Was this a normal byproduct of having two top-notch singers share the same space? Or did Reya actually harbor malevolent intent toward Carolina?

Carolina firmly closed the Crush Bus door and we strode off toward the midway area. We could hear excited shrieks sounding over the blaring rock music. Someone had definitely kicked up the volume on the rides tonight.

She took a deep breath. "Girl, it's been such a long time since we've hung out here together. Of course, we never got into any trouble at the fair, thanks to your bodyguard big brother...try as I might to flirt with the shady ride attendants."

I laughed. "Remember that last summer, when you got your hands on your mom's maroon lipstick and you'd sneak it on every time we went out?"

She groaned. "Yeah, it wasn't really my color, was it? And I still remember Bo telling me to wipe it off before we got out of the car."

"In all fairness, you *were* only eleven."

"Yeah, but I had my growth spurt early. You know I probably looked sixteen."

I grinned. "Exactly. That's why he told you to wipe it off."

As we neared the Ferris wheel, Carolina put on her baseball cap and pulled it down low. "I've learned that I can't be too careful, even at night," she said.

"I'll bet," I murmured, leading the way into the covered cart. We buckled in, and Carolina made no attempt to flirt with the wizened ride attendant who firmly latched our door.

As the carts rose into the air, Carolina let out a huge sigh. "What if I hadn't made it?" she asked.

She was likely still in shock that someone had poisoned her, and no wonder. I tilted my face into the pleasant breeze that was created as the ride picked up speed. "Who would've done that to you, Carolina? Have you talked with the police?"

"Detective Hatcher came by, and I told him my movements

that night. It seemed like there were plenty of opportunities for someone to tamper with my food."

"But did they ever tell you what poison was used? Surely that could help point the detective in the right direction."

She shook her head. "It turned out to be Digoxin. It's a medicine for abnormal heart rhythms and things like that. So I guess it's not some exclusive poison that's hard to get hold of, like cyanide. I'm guessing plenty of hotel guests use it. Anyway, it was good that they caught it when they did. If the dose had been just a little higher..."

"I'm guessing the poisoner miscalculated." I looked up at the sky as we reached the top. The stars were barely visible due to the bright fairground lights, but it was a clear night.

"Maybe," she admitted.

"Or else..." I needed to float another theory past Carolina, and it was one she might not care for. I cleared my throat. "Or else someone only wanted you to miss your fair performances."

She reacted as I knew she would, with total disbelief. "Are you insinuating that someone else wanted a moment in the sun?"

"Well, yes, I am."

She frowned. "I suppose you mean Reya, since she'd have to take my place?"

"I guess so." I hesitated. "Or what about Tony? Does he ever sing backup? Maybe he'd have to take center stage?"

"My husband," she mused, toying with a piece of hair. I could tell she was deep in thought.

The ride slowed. Raising her voice, Carolina spoke to the attendant. "Could you give us one more time around, please? There's no line."

The old man's leathery face broke into a toothless grin. "Happy to, ma'am."

The other riders clapped as the ride picked up speed.

Carolina's pensive look returned. "Tony *has* been acting weird, to be honest. He's been sort of...disdainful, maybe? Acting like I'm nothing to him. And he keeps disappearing on me—like tonight, when the rest of us were working on stuff in the bus."

My thoughts immediately jumped to Jake and how he'd acted when he cheated on me. He'd been insolent and secretive, especially in weeks leading up to his unexpected announcement that he was leaving me.

"Uh—I hate to ask, but is it possible Tony's seeing someone else?" When Carolina's eyes widened, I rushed to continue. "I know it sounds completely crazy, but I found out the hard way how easily husbands can hide their...indiscretions."

She made a dismissive motion with her hand. "No way. Tony's totally loyal—he's always been crazy about me. He couldn't hide something like that."

I fell silent, unwilling to argue with my friend. I hoped she was right. But hope was quick to vanish in the face of some types of facts.

Propping her chin on her hand, Carolina leaned against the side of the cart. I knew my words had struck home, even though she'd carelessly brushed them off.

Trying to lighten the mood, I said, "You have to stop by Barks & Beans sometime before you go. What day are you heading out?"

She straightened in her seat as the ride began to slow again. "We're doing two concerts—tomorrow and Sunday night—since the first one was postponed. So the plan is to leave on Monday. Staying at the Greenbrier isn't cheap, as you might've guessed." She gave a slow smile.

"I'm sure."

A text tone pinged and Carolina glanced at her phone. For the briefest of moments, her look hardened.

I was tempted to ask who'd texted, but obviously it was none of my business. Carolina seemed to have closed herself off for the evening, retreating somewhere into her own head. It was a talent she'd always possessed—the ability to remove herself from being completely present.

In silence, we exited onto the metal platform. I told the attendant thanks, and he gave us both a knowing grin. He must've worked out the fact that he'd given an extra ride to Carolina Garten herself.

"Do you always have that effect on people?" I asked, walking her back to the Crush Bus.

"I'm afraid so," she said. "When we started out, it was amazing—the success of that first album, the way it felt like everyone knew the lyrics to 'Not Forgotten.' But then the song got played out, and even I got sick of hearing it everywhere we went. Ever since then, we've had to come up with bigger and better songs, and it gets tiring chasing your own tail. Plus, it's so hard to go incognito anywhere. The photographers and fans are all over the place."

I couldn't relate in the slightest, but I gave a murmur of understanding. As we approached the tour bus, she stopped short and turned. The bodyguard stood silent sentry near the door.

"Listen, Macy, I appreciate all your help. I really do. I feel like Detective Hatcher will get to the bottom of the whole poisoning situation, and in the meantime, as you saw, bodyguards have been hired to watch out for me by the bus and outside my hotel room. But for my own mental health, I have to act like no one has ill will against me, you know? It's the only way I can function at the top of my game for the concert tomorrow."

I gave her a hug. "I understand. And don't worry, you'll be

amazing. Just make sure you get all the rest you need. Are you heading back to the Greenbrier soon?"

"Yes, just as soon as Gage and I figure out a few things. I think Murphy'll drive me over."

Although I wasn't convinced that Carolina was in good hands with anyone connected with the band, I had no right to demand she take more steps to be careful. That was her call, and like she said, she needed to focus all her energy on the concert tomorrow.

"I'll see you tomorrow night, then," I said.

"Oh, yes! I'm so glad you'll be there! I'll tell Murphy to text you where your seats are."

"I can't wait."

As I walked away, I recalled how rattled Carolina had looked after she got the text on the Ferris wheel. Who'd sent it, and what did it say?

Whether my friend wanted to admit it or not, someone had brazenly poisoned her, and it seemed likely it was someone she was close to.

I just hoped Carolina's concerts went off as planned, then she could load up and head home to Nashville. Maybe things would slip back into a routine and the poisoner would never again raise a hand against her.

But that seemed like a mighty big *maybe*.

6

As SOON AS my alarm rang, I peered out the window. The sky was already a deep blue, so it was probably going to be a great day for the concert.

After giving Coal some attention, I got dressed and went through the connecting door into the cafe—something I rarely used, except when there were no customers in the store. When Bo had renovated the front half of Auntie A's house as Barks & Beans, he'd left the back half for me to reside in. We'd worked together to paint and spruce it up, but I'd kept a lot of Auntie A's furniture, not minding that it was mismatched and well-used. Bo didn't live far away, in a modern, bungalow-style house just up the street—along with his kitten, Stormy.

I couldn't wait to get Stormy and Coal together again. Summer's suggestion that Bo might be a cat person had proven to be true, and last year he'd instantly fallen for the fluffy shelter kitten Summer had been fostering.

Bo and I had enjoyed no end of entertainment watching the fierce Calico kitten—now nearly a full-grown cat—as she swiped and hissed at my huge Dane, mostly because we'd realized Coal was genuinely fearful of her. Her larger-than-life attitude covered up for the glaring size difference between them.

Barks & Beans wasn't open yet, and I appreciated the relative silence as I walked in. I waved at Jimmy and Kylie, who were setting up the coffee area. Charity usually arrived a little later, once her grandson's sitter had showed up and she'd loaded up her baked goods. Her little guy would be starting school soon, I supposed.

I headed over to the Barks section and opened the low gate. The dog-petting area was my domain, and I liked to keep things tidy. Although Summer was fastidious about cleaning up the shelter dogs before they arrived, I did keep busy sweeping up stray hairs and picking up toys.

Thankfully, it looked like someone had already done that, so I used my time to unload a few dog foods and products onto the shelves. Summer arrived and dropped off a wiry-haired, medium-sized gray dog, along with a grizzled black Lab who was way past his prime.

"You seem to be getting quite a few older dogs. Is that a good or bad thing?" I asked, recalling a sweet dog named Edison we'd placed last winter with a lonely widow. He hadn't been long for this world, but it was a comfort knowing he'd be loved on for the rest of his days.

She patted the black dog's head. "Yeah, it's not the time of year when we get a lot of abandoned puppy litters. We have a few more cats than usual, but you don't want cats here...do you?" She gave me a hopeful look.

I hated to shut her down, but I shook my head. "Sorry, Summer. This is a dog-only venture—dogs are my thing, you know. That's why Bo concocted the Barks & Beans idea, to give me an opportunity to work with the animals I love. Doesn't your foster program cater to a lot of cat lovers?"

"Oh, yes, of course." She leaned down to unhook the dogs' leashes, then stood. "Cats are generally easier to care for, so yes, the foster program is great for them. Quite a few get placed that way. But if you ever want to do a cat day here, I'm sure we could work something out."

"You do know you're quite convincing when you want to be, Summer Adkins." I glanced over as the noise level rose in the cafe. Our first customers were arriving. "We'll talk about this later, I promise."

She adjusted the jaunty green silk scarf she'd tied on like a headband. "I hope that means we'll talk while going out to eat somewhere delicious."

"You got it." I grinned.

As Summer walked out, a woman wearing huge, oversized sunglasses and a loose bun strode in. Her white jeans were artistically ripped and her black tank top was knotted in the front. She wore beat-up black flip-flops. But I'd know that lanky build anywhere.

Since the younger dog was playing contentedly with a chew toy and the older dog was already falling asleep in a patch of sunlight, I opened the gate and walked over to say hello to my country star friend who looked anything like a star this morning.

Stepping up next to her in line, I whispered, "Carolina."

She turned, then gave me a quick side-hug. "Macy."

She looked and sounded exhausted. Surely the Digoxin should be totally out of her system by now? Maybe the concert prep was grueling.

"You doing okay?" I whispered, throwing a quick glance at the customers around us. So far, they seemed more preoccupied with deciding on a drink choice than with looking at Carolina.

"I'm not sure." Carolina took her place at the front of the

line and hesitated. "I can't make up my mind about anything, it seems," she muttered.

"How about I order for you?" I asked.

She nodded. "I'd love that. I trust your judgment."

I picked up one of Charity's raspberry streusel bars and asked Kylie if she'd make a foam art latte and bring it over to my friend's table. Kylie nodded, running Carolina's card before turning to make the espresso. She'd recently gotten her dark bob trimmed, so the dragon tattoo that wrapped up her neck and down her bare arms was on full display today. I found it interesting that Carolina didn't even look at the spectacular tattoo twice. Either she'd seen it all before in her music circles, or she was completely distracted today. Maybe a little of both.

I asked Jimmy if he'd mind stepping in with the dogs for a minute, and he was happy to oblige. Charity was already bustling about and the cafe wasn't very crowded, so I knew the two women could hold down the fort while I caught up with Carolina.

I led my friend to a private recessed area where an old chimney had been torn out. Now it was a white brick nook, the perfect size for the two-seater table Bo had positioned there. We settled into our chairs and I got right down to business.

"You're not doing well," I said. "And are you out alone?"

She didn't remove her dark glasses. "No, the bodyguard is outside. And no—I'm not doing great. But I had to stop in and see your cafe."

Kylie walked over and presented the latte to Carolina. As always, her art design elicited an immediate response. The foam featured a dolphin that looked nearly 3D as it leapt above an ocean wave.

"How'd you guess that I love the ocean?" Carolina asked. "This is amazing!"

I was impressed at Kylie's surprisingly intuitive choice.

When Carolina was younger, she'd always talked about becoming a marine biologist someday. I was sure her current career had turned out far more lucrative.

"Just seemed to fit. Thanks." Kylie walked off, the lug soles on her ever-present combat boots squeaking as she went.

Knowing my time was short, I asked, "Is anything going on?"

Carolina gave a tight smile. "Besides being the victim of a poisoning? As a matter of fact, yes. Last night was awful. When I got back to the Greenbrier, Tony was nowhere to be found. He wasn't answering my texts, either. Finally, I actually called him and he picked up. I could hear the noise in the background and I knew he was down at the casino."

She took a tiny bite of the streusel bar and continued. "See, the problem is, I recently found out Tony's in debt—*deep* debt. Back at home, when he started acting defensive, I made some calls to check on our accounts. I discovered that several credit cards he said he'd closed were still open—and he'd racked up hundreds of thousands of dollars' debt on them."

I didn't want to sound rude, but a band as big as Carolina Crush must be rolling in money. "Is that too much for you all to pay off?"

She shook her head. "Not on its own. But to add insult to injury, I picked up the mail the day before we traveled here and there was a letter from the bank addressed to Tony. I opened it, figuring it was an overdraft bill or something." She took a long sip of her latte and wiped foam from her upper lip. The cup trembled in her hand as she lowered it to the saucer. "It turned out to be a letter saying the bank was going to foreclose on our house. Tony was six months behind on payments on the mortgages *and* the home equity loans I didn't know he'd even taken out. Multiple mortgages." She shook her head.

"How did this happen without your knowledge?" I asked. "Didn't you co-sign for the house?"

"The house was only in his name—just to be on the safe side. Murphy recommended it because one of his clients got sued once and wound up having to leverage his house. He said it would be better if such a large asset wasn't in my name." She took a bigger bite of the streusel bar. "I guess we weren't staying on the safe side, after all."

"Don't kick yourself," I said. "Now you know why Tony was acting weird. Did you confront him on it?"

"Not at the time—I wanted to wait until the concerts were over and we were back home. I figured I could scrounge around and pay off the mortgages so the bank wouldn't foreclose. But then I realized Tony was downstairs gambling..."

"And you lost your temper?" I asked. One thing I'd learned early in our friendship was that although Carolina seemed pretty laid back, if you pushed her too hard on something she felt strongly about, she had a tendency to blow her top.

She dipped her head, staring at the dregs of her latte. "I did. I demanded that he come back to our suite. When he opened the door, I told him I knew all about the debts and the mortgages."

That was a risky move, because Tony could've been the one who'd tried to poison her. Her outburst could've ended up with her getting beaten up or far worse, if Tony was already inclined to get rid of his wife.

Maybe her dark glasses were hiding bruises...

"What happened then?" I demanded.

My urgent tone must've given away my suspicious thoughts. "Oh, he didn't hurt me or anything like that, Macy. But he did try to justify himself. He said he'd earned that money, so he could spend it however he wanted. Then he had to remind me that he'd come up with the name for the band, way back when. I figured he was just lashing out at me, but *then* he had the absolute audacity to say that he doubted if I could do one productive thing on my own, outside of showing off in front of a crowd." She finally took off her sunglasses and slammed them onto the table, heedless of the customers around us. Her eyes had dark circles under them, but nothing more. "Me. He said this to *me*. I'm his bread and butter. Without me, he's nothing."

I tried to calm her down. "Believe me when I say I understand. I've been lied to by a husband, too."

She shook her head. "Jerks. Well, I made him sleep on the couch. I don't know how I can go on sharing a room with him. I don't even know if I *want* to pay off his stupid debts. Maybe I should hang him out to dry."

One of the dogs yipped, signaling that I needed to get back. I pushed my chair back and stood. "Listen, if you need some space, why don't you come over and stay with me for a while? I have a couple of guest rooms and you'd be safe at my place."

She looked thoughtful. "You live in the back half of this house?"

"Yes, and trust me, that half looks a *whole* lot more like the house you remember."

She giggled. "Bright floral wallpaper and all?"

"We actually did take that down. I couldn't stand to look at that stuff every day." Placing a light hand on her shoulder, I said, "I want you to think about it, okay? Just let me know. You could come back to my place after the concert tonight. I'll make dinner or something." That *or something* left room for me to ask Bo to whip something up for us. I was not the best cook in the world.

"I will. I'll text you later on today," she said. She stood and shoved her glasses back on. "Thanks for talking, Macy. I'd love to spend time with the dogs, but I've stayed too long already."

We shared a quick hug before Carolina headed out. This time, I saw several customers watching her.

Her life was already hard enough, but now she'd had a blowout with Tony that had probably rocked her world, just like Jake's point-blank admission of his affairs and demand for a divorce had shocked me last January. I'd had no true friends in South Carolina when he'd dropped that bomb, and on top of that, Auntie A was dying with cancer and Bo lived in California. I would've loved to have had someone nearby who was standing in my corner. Maybe I could be that someone for Carolina in her time of need.

7

AFTER MY WORK SHIFT, I whirled through my house like a tornado, cleaning the downstairs bathroom and straightening the living room and kitchen in case Carolina decided to stay over for a while. I knew she had at least one other concert planned, and she seemed to enjoy being back at her old stomping grounds.

Coal sensed that something was up, so he trailed after me, looking slightly forlorn. Giving him a head pat, I assured him, "You'll like Carolina, boy. There's nothing to fret over."

As if getting the gist of what I was saying, he trudged over to his pillow and stretched out.

After letting him out a final time, I gave him plenty of food and water and locked up. The sun was starting to set, and we'd probably need to show up early to claim our seats at the concert. Murphy had sent me the online tickets, and I had a feeling we were going to be close to the stage.

By the time I got there, Bo had our booth all closed up and packed up. He'd also swung by the Greek foods booth and picked up a couple of gyros for us. We savored the exotic fare as we walked toward the stage. After dumping our paper plates in the trash can, we finagled our way through the packed bleachers and found our way to our seat numbers—which were smack in the middle of the very front rows.

"Track seating," Bo breathed. "I can't believe it."

Feeling fairly proud of my hot-shot connections, I beamed at him. "Believe it."

"I'm not even a country music fan, but I have to admit, their songs are catchy," he said. "Does Carolina write them?"

I shook my head. "I've read that Tony writes most of the lyrics." I fell silent, wondering how the band structure was going to change if Carolina decided to divorce her lying husband.

Backlights kicked on and the fog machine started pumping. People around us could hardly contain their excitement, waving their phones in the air and screaming. Reya was the first to take the stage, then Tony, then Gage. Finally, when the crowd had reached a deafening pitch, Carolina strode to the forefront.

I gasped. I'd never seen her in full-on country star mode, and she was impressive. Long eyelashes, red lipstick, and voluminous hair complemented her ensemble of leather shorts, a silver sequined blouse, and thick-soled, knee-high boots. When she opened her mouth to sing, she was absolutely breathtaking. The crowd fell silent, soaking it all in.

By the time they started the quieter second song, I was able to put a finger on a sound that didn't quite mesh. Tony's dulcimer timing was off. Not *way* off, but definitely off. I wondered if something was wrong with his headset or maybe even the instrument itself. Or maybe Tony was still reeling from his blowout with Carolina.

It didn't really matter, because my old friend was on the top of her game. As she belted out "Not Forgotten," which was by

far her most popular song, the crowd joined in. I had to look
twice when I heard Bo chime in beside me. My brother had
always been a bit of an enigma, and this just confirmed it.
Somewhere along the way, he'd actually learned the lyrics for a
country song. As I pondered the words, which were a lament to
lost love, I had the sinking feeling that he was thinking about
Tara.

All I knew is that I'd never sing that song thinking of Jake
the Snake. I could only dream that I *would* one day be able to
forget my ex.

Carolina wasn't much of a dancer, but her long, lean legs
allowed her to take impressive strides as she stalked along the
front of the stage. Gage stayed in roughly the same circle of
space, but he moved closer to Carolina for their duets.

Reya, who was wearing a knockout red cocktail dress,
occasionally stepped forward to sing backup. In fact, she came
so far forward for one song, it was obvious she was trying to
capture more of the spotlight than Carolina.

The spotlight went down and the backlights flipped to
purple. As the instruments quieted, the audience fell silent.
When the lights came up, Carolina was sitting on a wooden
stool to the left, an acoustic guitar strapped over her shoulder.
I'd totally forgotten that Gage wasn't the only guitar player in
the band—and it seemed everyone else had, too. As Carolina
strummed a couple of cords, the crowd's anticipation was
palpable. Was she about to debut an entirely new song, one
without her standard backup music?

She stood and played a haunting melody, then reached for
the mic. The moment her fingers touched it, a sound like a
gunshot rang out and a blue light arced into the air.

The crowd gave shouts of confusion as Carolina tumbled
onto the stage, her arms splayed wide.

Gage rushed to Carolina's side, with Reya and Tony close

behind. Murphy appeared from behind the stage, shouting for someone to call an ambulance.

Bo sprang into action, forcing a path through the three rows ahead of us. He clambered onto the stage and rushed past Gage, who was frantically checking for Carolina's pulse. Without slowing, Bo jogged straight toward the soundboard and unplugged it.

By the time Bo turned back toward Carolina, Gage had found a pulse. He gave a thumbs-up to the crowd. Quite a few fans started crying. I was still frozen in place, trying to understand what had just happened.

The crowd parted as two bodyguards raced up the side aisles and converged on the stage. Although they were wearing jeans to try to blend in, it was clear they were wearing headsets. They spoke to the band members and had them form a circle around Carolina to shield her from view. Then the guards positioned themselves in front of the band, tucking in their shirts to reveal previously concealed pistols.

Bo spoke with one of them, and the man nodded. I wasn't surprised when my brother took up a position by the stage steps, adjusting his button-up shirt to reveal his own Glock. He went almost everywhere with his concealed weapon.

A siren screamed as an ambulance made its way through the grass, parking near the stage. Gesturing wildly at the EMTs, Murphy lurched down the steps to meet them.

I glanced around, trying to get a feel for the crowd. Would they leave or stick around until Carolina was off the stage? Given the number of upraised phones, it was safe to assume this event had already been splashed onto social media.

After giving Carolina a fast check, EMTs moved her onto a stretcher and down the stairs. Soon after, the bodyguards led Murphy and the rest of the band members offstage. The somber group walked around back, presumably to gather in the Crush Bus.

The crowd started scattering. I'd lost sight of Bo, so I sat down to wait for him and try to collect my thoughts. Given the huge blue spark, the loud boom, and the way Bo had rushed directly over to the soundboard, I assumed Carolina had gotten a severe shock. Anger wormed its way through me, setting my arms shaking. Surely this was a deliberate act of sabotage.

A clammy hand dropped on my shoulder. "Macy Hatfield, is that you?"

I whirled around. Mattie Conley, childhood bully extraordinaire, stood staring at me. Her hulking husband Aidan was by her side, but his gaze was fixed somewhere in the distance, maybe watching the band.

"Yes, it's me," I said stupidly, fervently wishing this encounter away.

She nodded. "I thought so. I heard you were back in town. You're running that dog shop with your brother, right?"

I stood, but I still felt small next to the tall couple. "Actually, it's a dog cafe. We bring shelter dogs in so customers can spend time—"

"Oh, honey." She pressed her perfectly manicured dark green nails to her heart. "I'm not a dog person *at all*." She leaned back into Aidan's wide chest. "And neither is my husband here, are you?"

Aidan gave a monosyllabic answer that could've meant anything. He pushed his dark, messy bangs straight up with his thick hand and stared at the stage.

Mattie leaned in. "I just wanted to find out your secret— how'd you manage to get these amazing seats? I mean, we were online the day the tickets released, and they booked up so *fast*."

It was the glorious opening I'd always dreamed of—a chance to rub my success in Mattie's face. I pulled myself up to my full five foot three height and angled my chin jauntily. "You might not remember, but Carolina and I were always good friends." This stood in contrast to Mattie, who'd probably forgotten the time she'd stuck her foot out and made Carolina's bike flip over, so she'd had to wear an arm cast for weeks.

"Of course I remember." Mattie huffed. "Honestly, I wasn't asking for myself. Aidan likes their music far more than I do. I find it far too repetitive." She grabbed Aidan's arm and stormed off.

"What was up with them?" Bo asked. He'd sauntered up to my side, seeming none the worse for wear after his heroic action of the evening.

I sank onto a bench, feeling exhausted on Carolina's behalf. "I have no idea. Mattie's always been queen of her own world, so I guess she doesn't like the fact that Carolina's gone and eclipsed her."

"That was Mattie from grade school? *The* Mattie you were always telling me about?" He sat down next to me.

I sighed. "The very one. And you know the most telling thing of all? She didn't even talk about what happened to Carolina tonight. All she cared about was finding out how we landed our stupid seats." I stood to walk back to my car and Bo also got to his feet. "What *did* happen on stage? Was it a shock? Is she going to be okay? She was supposed to come and stay with me, and now I don't know what's going to happen."

Bo placed a comforting hand on my shoulder before going on to answer my rapid-fire questions in his typical gentle fashion. "Yes, it was a shock—though not 'electrocution,' which some news sites are already saying. Electrocution means you were shocked *to death*. What happened is that the instant she touched the mic, the electricity ran through her and completed the circuit with the guitar, which was plugged into an amplifier. The cords connected back at the soundboard, which is why I went straight over and unplugged that." He gestured back toward the stage, where the bodyguards had once again taken up their positions. "They're securing the area until Detective Hatcher gets here with his people," he explained. "I'm sure he'll find out if someone tampered with the wires."

"I feel positive that someone did." I kicked at a dirt clod as we passed the stables, where a couple of horses were nickering. It was probably their feeding time. Sadness flooded me as I recalled my offer to make Carolina supper after the concert. I hoped she wasn't feeling hungry on top of everything else.

Bo, whose long legs had easily outpaced my short strides, stopped and turned. His blue gaze was charged with compassion. "Listen, sis. I know you're worried. I've asked Murphy to update us as to her condition. But I do think she'll be okay. One of her bodyguards said she was verbally responsive by the time they got her to the ambulance. The other dude said it was a good thing she'd worn those rubber-soled boots tonight and not heels, like she often wears for concerts."

She had worn showstopper boots, their soles nearly platform-thick. Thank goodness she'd chosen those, probably to show off her lean legs. In a way, maybe her vanity had saved her.

"She was having trouble with her husband," I volunteered, hitting the unlock button on my key fob as we approached our vehicles. "That's why she wanted to leave the Greenbrier."

"Makes sense," Bo mused, opening my car door for me and leaning against it as I slid into the driver's seat. "I'm sure she'll be in the hospital overnight, but maybe tomorrow you can check in on her and see when she'll get out."

I pulled the door shut and rolled down my window. The thick, warm air of the fair rushed in to fill my car. It was a curious concoction of popcorn, hot dogs, and caramel, mingled with the very human scent of something I could only describe as undiluted excitement. "Thanks for walking me back, Bo," I said. "Guess I'll see you for church in the morning?"

We still attended the church we'd grown up in. I sang soprano in the choir, and I didn't like to miss a moment with that uplifting group of ladies.

"Sure thing. I'll pick you up at the regular time."

I flipped on my parking lights and waited for Bo to get into his big white truck, then I pulled out and led the way to our street. Sometimes I wondered if it was weird that my brother and I did a lot of things together, but really, it made all kinds of sense. Our parents had died when I was only two and Bo was six. Auntie A had adopted us, but we'd always leaned on each other for support...at least until Bo left to join the Marines. His exit from home sent me on a lonely tailspin when I wound up making some bad decisions...like marrying Jake before my family had even met him.

Then last year, we'd both suffered crushing blows when our significant others—my husband and Bo's fiancée—walked out on us. Now, in hindsight, I could see how those blows had led to a much better job situation for both of us as co-owners of the Barks & Beans Cafe. But no matter how much time had passed, we were both still grieving our losses.

I'd left my back porch light on, so I walked the garden path quickly and unlocked the door. Instead of blasting right past me to use the bathroom, Coal instead sidled up and leaned heavily against my leg, begging to be petted. I smoothed the soft fur on his forehead, tears welling in my eyes. "You know what, boy? You're my daily reminder that everything works out for the best." I stooped to press a kiss on his big head.

8

A<small>FTER</small> <small>CHURCH</small>, Bo asked if I wanted to come to his place for Sunday dinner. I was only too happy to take him up on the offer. As usual, I had nothing planned. But first I needed to call the hospital and check on Carolina, since Murphy hadn't updated us yet. I asked Bo to come in and keep Coal occupied while I went into another room to talk. Then we could walk Coal over to Bo's house so he could hang out with his feline frenemy.

After receiving a royal brush-off from the hospital, I realized it was a mistake to call them at all. Of *course* Carolina's privacy needed to be protected at all costs—for all I knew, her fans could've set up camp in the lobby and held an all-night vigil for her recovery. The hospital certainly wouldn't be handing out information. But I didn't want to call Carolina directly.

I tried another tack and called Detective Hatcher. When he picked up—obviously in the middle of a meal with his family —I felt awful. But he said it wasn't an inconvenience at all. While he couldn't say much since it was an open investigation, he was able to tell me that Carolina was stable and even eating some. He'd spoken with her early this morning and she'd told him she was planning to leave the Greenbrier and stay with me for a while. "She's anxious to get out," he said. "You could probably text her soon."

I hung up, feeling immensely relieved. After relaying the good news to Bo, I texted Carolina and told her she was welcome to come stay with me anytime.

Coal was excited to go on the leash, and we headed up the sidewalk to Bo's place, basking in the early-afternoon sunshine. I glanced at the large house next to mine and realized something had changed.

Nudging Bo, I pointed at the lawn. "Look! The *For Sale* sign is gone. You think someone bought the old Pettrey place?"

Bo squinted. "Yes, I'm guessing so. Hasn't it been up for sale around seven months?"

"Right—they listed it soon after old man Pettrey died. No one in his family wanted to keep it."

"It'll take some work, that's for sure. When I went to visit him, I noticed that a lot of the old plaster is cracking up. But it's a gorgeous old Colonial like Auntie A's, and it has original wood floors."

Coal started sniffing his way toward the neighboring house, probably sensing we were curious about it. I gave a light tug on his leash. "C'mon boy, let's go see Stormy."

As we reached Bo's front porch, I got a return text from Carolina. After reading it, I turned to Bo. "I can't stay too long, unfortunately. Carolina's getting out in a couple of hours and she'll get to my house around three. She said she's feeling okay, but says she'd like to walk around town, just to get her feet under her a little better."

"Will you need food tonight?" Bo asked, pushing open his ocean blue front door. The light and airy interior of his quaint bungalow reflected a beachy theme. That was one thing I was sure Bo missed—being so close to the ocean. Here in West Virginia, it took hours to reach the Atlantic. Bo wasn't quite the woods-loving child of the mountains I was.

"We'll be good. Carolina said something about stopping to eat. Although I have no idea where we can go, given that she's so famous."

"She seems to have learned how to cope with it." Bo tossed his keys on his kitchen island. In typical cat fashion, Stormy didn't make a move to greet us. Instead, she did a back stretch on her perch near the window and shot Coal a deadly glare as he bumbled in behind me.

Stormy was a beautiful long-haired Calico with captivating green eyes. She had a cute black patch that stretched along one side of her nose. She wasn't yet a year old, but her tornado-like frisking tactics had died down a little over the past couple of months.

She idly batted a jingling kitty ball off her cat tower. I could swear she was daring Coal to try to take it. Knowing my boy wouldn't even touch one of her things, I unleashed him.

After shooting me a hesitant backward glance, Coal attempted to tiptoe into the living room to join Stormy. Her hair spiked a little and her tail fluffed up.

"Calm down, Stormy." Bo walked over to her. "You know he's not going to hurt you."

Feeling slightly offended, I said, "More like the other way around."

Bo grinned. "I don't think she'll hurt him, either." He picked her up and carried her closer to Coal, who had decided to lie down. Sure enough, the bold kitty couldn't resist stretching a paw out toward him.

"Is she trying to scratch him?" I demanded.

"No—I think she wants to play with him," Bo said.

He gingerly set Stormy down. In a blink, she leapt right over Coal, then batted her jingle ball back toward him. Skittering back to the shelter of her tower, she crouched and waited for him to return the toy.

Coal gave me an utterly forlorn look which plainly said he didn't speak kitty language.

I got on the floor and tapped the ball back toward Stormy. "See? She wants the ball."

Bo walked over to his fridge and started taking food out to prepare lunch. "They'll figure it out, sis," he said over his shoulder.

Sure enough, Coal crawled forward a tiny bit and nudged the ball with his nose. It didn't roll far, but Stormy darted from her safe spot and bopped the ball right back.

I'd never been one for games, but this one was going to be endlessly entertaining to watch.

I LINGERED after eating so our pets could hang out a while longer. By the time I was ready to go, Stormy had curled up next to Coal's head and gone to sleep.

"Let me know if you need anything," Bo said, picking Stormy up so Coal would finally stand. "You're on duty at the booth tomorrow with Kylie and Charity, right?"

"Yes, I am. And you enjoy your day at the cafe. Oh—and don't think I've forgotten about your date with Summer. I still have a hundred questions, but I'm saving up for when we have lots of time to talk."

He gave me a mischievous smile. "But what if I don't want to answer you?"

I smirked. "You know I'll get everything out of Summer, anyway."

"Yeah, no doubt." He waved, and Coal and I headed down the stairs. I looked forward to seeing how Carolina was doing, but I knew she still had to be hurting on multiple levels. A walk around the quaint town of Lewisburg would be just what the doctor ordered.

THE DOORBELL RANG and I shushed Coal before he could give one of his booming warning barks. "It's okay," I said, opening the door for Carolina.

She stood on my porch, toting a rose-gold rolling suitcase in each hand. She wobbled a little as I reached out to pull her into a big hug. "I'm so sorry this happened to you," I said. "Are you feeling okay?"

"I'm kind of fuzzy-headed and my toes and fingers keep tingling, but outside of that, I'm alright. They told me that those clunky black boots might've saved my life."

"You made a wise fashion choice last night. Come on in."

Recognizing that I knew Carolina, Coal maintained a polite distance as he stood in the living room. I gestured toward him. "Meet my own rescue dog—his name is Coal. Remind me to tell you the story of how I got him sometime."

Carolina gave him a once-over. "He's *huge*. How much does he weigh?"

"Around 165 now, I think, but I'm not sure—he hasn't visited the vet in a while."

She nodded. "You always did like your dogs."

Taking one of her suitcases, I led her down the hall to the guest room. "You'll be in here—there's a bathroom attached. Coal sleeps upstairs in my room, so he won't be any bother."

She looked at the queen-size bed covered with one of Auntie A's wedding ring quilts and accented with lots of velvet throw pillows. "This looks like heaven after the hospital," she said, kicking off her shoes.

"I doubt it competes with the Greenbrier."

After dropping her suitcase, she fell back on the bed and squeezed a red pillow tight. "Quite the contrary. I was ready to get out of there. I didn't care how beautiful our suite was—I couldn't stand to be with Tony another minute. And I convinced Detective Hatcher I'd be safest staying *away* from the band at your place, so now the bodyguards will only be on duty when I'm at the bus or on stage."

I sat down next to her. "Yeah...but don't you think your onstage shock could have been an open attempt to kill you? I mean, has anyone been acting weird lately, outside of Tony?"

She gave a mirthless laugh. "Sometimes I wonder if anyone *isn't* acting weird on this trip. Reya keeps trying to inject herself into songs that don't require her vocals. Murphy's been pressuring me to come up with another hit like 'Not Forgotten.' Tony—well, you know how he's been. And Gage is just kind of distant, which is strange because usually he's the life of the party."

"Woman troubles?" I asked, still wondering if the rumors that he liked Carolina were true.

She shook her head. "Gage hasn't been in a serious relationship in years. He claims that being single helps his muse." She slowly sat up and pulled on a shoe. "I don't know about you, but I need some exercise. How about we take our walk now, then you pick a place to eat? I think there are quite a few new restaurants I haven't tried yet."

"Okay, but only if you're *sure* you're okay to be walking around so soon." I stood. "Wait—I have an idea! You like art galleries, right? My friend Dylan has one you have to visit. He's always curating the best pieces. His place is called The Discerning Palette."

She grinned. "What a clever name for an art gallery! Plus he's an art-lover. He sounds like a winner. Are you interested in this Dylan fellow, by any chance?"

I couldn't restrain my nervous blush. "No, I mean—well, we're friends. I mean, he's quite handsome and all that, but I'm just not—"

Despite her recent full-body shock, her blue eyes were sharp. "You like someone else," she observed.

I sighed. "I don't know. Maybe." Titan McCoy, my brother's FBI agent friend, had somehow infiltrated a lot of my thoughts lately, even though we hadn't been in contact for months.

She giggled, and it felt like we were ten years old again. "And now you're going to have to tell me all about your mystery man."

9

DYLAN WAS THRILLED to see us come in and gave us a personal gallery tour to show off his latest pieces. I could tell Carolina was instantly enthralled with him—she'd always had a soft spot for men who seemed to belong to the intelligentsia.

Today he wore a plaid charcoal blazer, striped tie, and dark jeans. As usual, his collar-length dark hair looked artfully disheveled, and he wore the dark-framed glasses he only used at work. From his cavalier manner, I wasn't sure if he recognized Carolina, but he wasn't a country music fan, so it was possible he had no idea who she was.

Once we said goodbye and got out of earshot, Carolina said, "He's really into you."

I stopped short. "You think so?" Sure, Dylan kept asking me out, but I figured it was simply because we had a lot in common. I hadn't perceived that he harbored particularly strong feelings toward me.

"Of course. He was sneaking glances your way the whole time he was talking to me." She chuckled. "Plus, he didn't even respond to my friendliness. It's rare that people don't know who

I am. I have to say it's so *refreshing* to meet men in the wild like that."

I laughed. "Yeah, Dylan's a fan of classical music. He goes to the Carnegie Hall concerts in town. I doubt he's ever heard of Carolina Crush."

"So he's an art nerd," she said. "And his cleft chin—it's so Henry Cavill. Are you sure you don't have even a *little* crush on him?"

"Stop trying to set me up," I said. "Honestly, I'm not looking for a relationship right now."

"That wasn't how it sounded when you told me about Mister McCoy."

We'd arrived at the restaurant. It served regional dishes like brown beans and cornbread, the kinds of comfort foods I figured Carolina needed today. "C'mon in," I said, hoping she'd drop the subject of my possible love interests. "You're going to like this place."

We took our time eating, reminiscing over hilarious escapades from our childhood. I suddenly recalled the run-in with Mattie at the fair and told Carolina all about it.

Her eyes sparked. "That regular harpy! So she swooped in to find out how you got your seats and didn't give a flying fig about me getting knocked out? Sounds about right. Once a bully, always a bully, I guess."

"She married that Aidan Conley—remember him? The big kid who was several grades ahead of us. I should ask Bo if he knew him."

She shook her head. "I've tried to block out a lot of things about growing up here. You remember how tight money was for my family. Dad turned our lives upside down when he moved us to Tennessee, but it was worth it, because we finally hit middle class status."

I recalled that Carolina had a baby brother who'd just started crawling right before they moved. "How's Claude doing?" I asked. "Is he in Tennessee, too?"

She sipped her water. "He is. He's in his own place now, but he's kind of...aimless, you know? He does odd jobs, but nothing to really stay on top of his bills." She slathered butter on her wedge of cornbread. "I've been helping him make his rent payments, just for now. Tony would be angry if he found out." She leaned in. "In fact, Tony would be furious if he knew that I left *any* of my estate to Claude in my will. Of course, Tony gets the bulk of it, being my husband, but Claude gets a good chunk, too."

My mind instantly flew to Carolina's recent brushes with death. Someone had definitely tried to poison her, and they might have attempted to electrocute her, too. Was her will some kind of motivating factor?

Tony would get the bulk of the estate and probably the rights to Carolina's music, too. Those songs would make money for years to come, and Tony could use that windfall to dig out of debt.

I doubted that Carolina's baby brother Claude had any driving motivation to kill her, no matter how shiftless he was. He was probably just the kind of person who didn't like to plan ahead. I had the strong sense that whoever was trying to harm Carolina was a planner, and a ruthless one at that.

I'd just swallowed a delicious bite of potato salad when I heard a familiar voice. Sheldia Powers, the local librarian, had made her way to our booth. From the way her large blue eyes shone, I knew she'd recognized Carolina.

After letting her gush for a few moments about Carolina's latest songs, I interrupted and asked how things were going with foster care. When I'd last seen her in December, the single woman had gotten her first foster child placement, a young boy.

Thrilled to share, Sheldia gave us the rundown on the three children she'd fostered since that time. She was extremely animated, heightening the effect of her Snow White coloring as her pale cheeks grew pink. She was thinking of adopting her current placement—a little girl.

When Carolina politely asked how she could help, Sheldia was only too happy to hand her a card with links to the foster care backpack program she ran at the library. After saying she hoped Carolina enjoyed her visit, Sheldia abruptly asked if she'd run into Aidan Conley yet.

Carolina shook her head. "No, but Macy saw him and his wife Mattie at my concert. Why?"

Sheldia pursed her rosebud lips. "Well, I was listening in on these construction workers at the library last month—they're renovating a wing—and one of them said that their co-worker, Aidan Conley, must've flipped out when he found out Carolina Crush was coming to town. The guy said Aidan was downright obsessed with your band. This guy went on to say that he'd gone over to Aidan's place once, and his man cave in the basement was covered with signed memorabilia, in particular pictures of the lead singer."

Carolina's eyes darted to the door. I knew she was ready to escape.

I hurried to the rescue. "Thanks for visiting with us, Sheldia. We'd better get the bill and walk on home. Carolina's had a long day and it's getting dark. It was good to see you again."

Sheldia gave an awkward nod. "I didn't get to ask how Barks & Beans is doing...and your brother? How is he?" She couldn't disguise the hopeful note in her voice. Sheldia had gone to school with Bo, and he'd stood up to bullies for her more than once. It was obvious she'd had a crush on him for years.

"We're all doing well," I said noncommittally. "Be sure to stop in sometime so your foster daughter can see the dogs."

"She'd love that. Will do." Sheldia ambled off.

Carolina seemed to be lost in thought. I knew Sheldia's remarks about Aidan bothered her.

Hoping for a distraction, I said, "Did you know that there was a bank truck heist in town last November? And did you further know that I still suspect our cheery librarian Sheldia stole some of the money that went missing?"

Carolina perked up. "You're kidding me. Her? She seemed totally harmless."

"Maybe she is, but she is *very* passionate about keeping her Bookmobile bus up and running. They still haven't found all the money." I placed my napkin on the table. "Now let's get you on home—I'll brew you a strong cup of decaf coffee in my French press, how about that?"

"Sounds perfect. And I have another good idea." She flagged the waiter. "We'll need two pieces of butterscotch pie to go, please." Turning back to me, she said, "Thank you for this relaxing evening, Macy. You don't know how much I needed a normal night like this in my life. You were always good to look out for me. I'm so glad that some people never change."

AFTER NIBBLING at her pie and drinking just a few sips of decaf, Carolina declared that she needed to go to bed. "I still feel pretty worn out," she said. "Maybe I overdid it. The doctor told me to take it easy, but I was so desperate to get off that stupid hospital bed." She reached out to pat Coal's head, and he obligingly took a step closer to bridge the space between them. "He's a good dog," she murmured. "Maybe I should get one."

"Dogs are good company," I said. "But it might be hard when you had to go on tours."

"If I got a small one, it could stay in the Crush Bus with me."

I walked her to her room. "Good point. Well, you know I can hook you up if you're interested in adopting one. The shelter gets all sizes. But am I right in thinking you're heading out before long? Are you doing another concert?"

"We scheduled one for tomorrow night, and I still hope to do it. Murphy said I can cancel if I don't feel like I can handle it, but I think a good night's sleep on your homey guest bed will do me no end of good. Plus, we'll have people triple-check the wiring before we go onstage. There's no way I'm picking up a guitar, and I'll use my wireless mic."

"Sounds like a good plan. Get some sleep." I closed the door behind her. Coal padded along after me as I locked up and headed for the stairs.

I changed clothes, then curled up with a book so I could wind down. Coal settled onto his large pillow and quickly conked out, probably exhausted from playtime with Stormy.

As I flipped to the page where I'd left off, my mind wandered back to the conversation with Sheldia. I was happy to hear that fostering was going well for her. But something else she'd said had raised some serious concerns, at least in my mind. Aidan Conley was obsessed with Carolina Crush—or, more specifically, with Carolina herself. He'd been at the concert the night she was shocked. Had he slipped away from Mattie, then crept onto the stage when the lights went down and tampered with the cords?

While I knew crazed fans sometimes attempted to kill the unattainable object of their obsession, was Aidan really that unhinged? From what I'd read, celebrity stalkers often spent years trying to gain personal recognition from a star—and they'd settle for good or bad recognition.

While it was true that Aidan had obtained a lot of signed memorabilia from the band, Carolina didn't seem to recognize his name. If he'd made any kind of threats along the way, I was sure that Murphy or her bodyguards would've flagged him as a potential danger—especially knowing they were traveling to his hometown.

Of course, sometimes things fell through the cracks. I really wished Carolina would rethink giving a final concert tomorrow night, but I knew if she was feeling up to it, there'd be no stopping her. It made sense, too—fans had already paid for tickets, and it would be a regular triumph story to see Carolina take the stage so soon after being shocked.

I only hoped that if someone did engineer that shock in order to kill Carolina, they wouldn't return to finish what they'd started.

10

Fog coated the fairground as I pulled into the parking lot. It was so heavy, I couldn't even see a car's length in front of me.

Kylie had already started setting up. Her messy bob looked like she hadn't slept well, and her outfit looked like something she'd thrown together in the dark—an oversized rock band tank top that might've done double duty as a nightgown, and denim flared crop pants that could more accurately be described as culottes.

I looked closely at her, noting that she was only wearing her eyeliner today. Usually she sported a veritable rainbow of eyeshadow colors, as well.

"What's up?" I asked.

She turned tired hazel eyes to me. "Just having some issues with my sister," she said.

I didn't speak, figuring she'd share more if she wanted to. Kylie wasn't the most outgoing of employees, and I knew she hadn't yet warmed to me as she had to Bo. They both had the same battle-hardened air about them. I knew nothing about Kylie's private life.

As she wiped out the steel filter, she elaborated a tiny bit. "My younger sister's living with me. She didn't come home on time, so I had to go and get her."

Something told me this sister-retrieval story was a real doozy, but I refused to let my curiosity get the best of me. "I'm glad you got her back," I said. "What's her name?"

Kylie stared at me like she'd been cornered. "Chelsea," she said finally.

A customer appeared, so she hurried to help him. I was elated that I'd managed to chip away at some of the impenetrable wall Kylie maintained around herself. I held the fleeting hope that maybe we'd get to be good friends.

But watching her stiff body language as she steamed the milk for the man's cappuccino, I knew that was wishful thinking.

CHARITY ARRIVED, and with her came a bevy of pastries and lunch sandwiches. The day seemed to move swiftly after that, largely because I was getting faster at making the coffee drinks. Maybe I was a little more confident when I wasn't under Bo's watchful eye...or else I was making mistakes and no one was catching me.

It could be that.

When business slowed, I decided to take an early lunch break. After finishing up one of Charity's turkey, bacon, and provolone sandwich on grilled Ciabatta bread, I walked past the kids' rides and headed for the cattle barns. I felt like revisiting memories of my childhood trips to the fair. The familiar whoosh of hay and hot air—tinged with just a bit of manure—hit me when I walked in. Some of the large animals were fairly intimidating up close, but all of them were well behaved and immaculately groomed since they were there to be shown. After making casual conversation with a couple of the owners, I wandered out.

I walked in to see the display quilts and was blown away by the craftsmanship, but I didn't really need to buy a new one. Glancing at my phone, I hurried out to catch the nostalgic ride on the Spider I'd promised myself.

The blazing sun beat down everyone in line, and to make matters worse, a couple of amorous twenty-something guys started hitting on me. One of them managed to slide into my cart at the very last minute, and I could smell alcohol oozing from his pores. Really? Drunk at this time of day? I scooted to the end of my seat and held onto the side as the carts lifted into the air. It would be a wonder if the dude didn't puke all over me.

The carts started flipping around, faster and faster, and I held my breath, hoping the drunk punk would somehow keep it together. Although he tried making a couple of advances, I shut them down so fast, he could only sit there gaping at me. It was obvious he wasn't so brave when he was alone. As the ride finally swirled to a stop, I jumped over the locked door and stalked off before the attendant came over to let us out. I hadn't even been able to enjoy my favorite ride.

Since there were about ten minutes left on my break, I decided to catch a ride on the Ferris wheel. When my turn came to get into the cart, I asked the attendant if I could ride alone. The young woman snapped her bubble gum and said, "Whatever you want, lady."

There was nothing that topped the slow, bird's eye view of the fairgrounds and surrounding areas. Sure, the grass was a little dry and the leaves weren't as green this time of year, but the mountains in the distance were still beautiful.

As my cart moved downward, I caught sight of a couple

that seemed like they were trying to hide behind the Bingo tent. I recognized the dark roots and platinum hair of Reya Heres, even though she'd swept it into a ponytail.

The man was on the short side and slim, with a dark beard and sunglasses. I looked closer, realizing it was Tony Garten.

My cart jolted and started its upward climb again. Their discussion seemed to dissolve into an argument. Reya shouted something I couldn't hear over the din of music that blared from the surrounding rides. Tony grabbed her arm in what was clearly a too-tight grip and yelled directly in her face. As she shouted right back at him, he let go, but he still looked irate. Surely someone would hear them and come to Reya's aid?

My cart topped the ride, forcing me to lose sight of them. I waved at the attendant, hoping she'd get the idea that I needed to disembark. Instead, she simply gave me a brief salute and the carts went around at least three more times.

Just before the Ferris wheel stopped, I caught sight of Tony hurrying toward the horse stables. My lunch break was definitely over, but I felt I should follow him to see what he was up to after arguing so violently with Reya. Ducking behind the rides so the Barks & Beans crew wouldn't see me, I hightailed it over toward the arena where the harness racing was happening later today. I had just rounded a corner when I bumped straight into the bulky form of Jimmy, our employee. He was walking hand in hand with his wife Jenny.

I launched into profuse apologies, but they both assured me that it could happen to anyone since things were so crowded today.

"But where were you off to, going so fast?" Jimmy asked. "Getting something from the car?"

"I was just checking...say, Jimmy—you're into horses, right? They're having harness races before the concert tonight, aren't they?"

"Sure are, miss. And some mighty fine horses are competing this year."

I had a stroke of insight. "Do people bet on the races?"

He shook his head. "Betting's not allowed, though I'm sure some is done under the table." His eyes sparkled. "Have you ever seen the horses up close? They're beautiful animals."

Knowing my trail toward Tony was growing colder by the second, I grasped for a way to catch up to him.

"No, but I'll go right over and check them out."

Jenny, a sprightly woman with bright red sunglasses and dyed blonde hair, grinned at her husband. "Jimmy, why don't you take Miss Hatfield over, and be sure to show her that gorgeous stallion. I want to pick up a lemonade, and I'll get you one, too. Meet you over in the West Virginia building?"

Jimmy nodded and I led the way to the stables, hoping to catch a glimpse of Tony. As we walked, Jimmy explained that the harness race horses were mostly Standardbreds, which had great speed and stamina and were good-natured. When we reached the first stable, I scanned the building, desperate to catch Tony in some underhanded act. But he wasn't around.

Jimmy walked me over to a large stall and greeted the man sitting near it. As I drew a little closer, a sudden neigh from inside made me jump. A sleek chestnut horse trotted over, apparently hoping for a treat.

"Isn't he a beauty?" Jimmy's gaze was fixed on the spectacular horse. "This is Chancellor. He's expected to win today."

Chancellor certainly was friendly. His nostrils flared like he was sniffing at my hair. I resisted the strong urge to pet his silky-looking nose, figuring that wasn't something visitors were supposed to do.

As we made our way toward the other side of the barn, I quietly asked, "Who owns him? That man sitting back there?"

Jimmy shook his head. "Oh, no, not him. Chancellor's owner is rarely seen in public. But he always pays for the best equipment and riders, and word on the street is that he moves in the highest circles. Only a handful of people know who he is, and I'm afraid I'm not one of them." He grinned.

The highest circles...would Tony Garten, a Carolina Crush band member, be considered to be in the highest circles? Probably by some, regardless of his toppling load of debt. Had he bought Chancellor?

Jimmy started toward the next stable, but I stopped him. "Thanks for introducing me to Chancellor. But Jenny's waiting for you over in the West Virginia building, and the ice is going to start melting in your lemonade. Plus, I need to get back to work. You go on ahead."

Wiping sweat from his forehead, Jimmy nodded. "I believe I will. You get yourself something cold to drink when you get back to the booth, too, Miss Hatfield." He lumbered off.

I didn't have enough time to zip through the other stables in hopes of finding Tony. By now, he was likely lounging in the air-conditioned Crush Bus.

As I approached our iced coffee booth, I was surprised to see Bo hurrying toward me. He wasn't even supposed to be here today.

"What're you doing here?" I asked.

His chin jutted out and he crossed his arms. Uh-oh, my brother was angry. Yes, my lunch break had gone over, and yes, Summer had already arrived with the shelter dogs, but—

"Where were you?" he demanded.

I slipped directly into scolded little sister mode. "What's it to you?"

He came closer, dropping his voice. "Did you just come from the stables?"

What was going on here? "Why, is there some kind of law

against visiting the stables? I ran into Jimmy, and he showed me the harness racing horses."

Bo's arms dropped and he relaxed a little. "Oh, so Jimmy was there. That's fine." He turned and started walking away.

I grabbed his arm. "What's going on? Why are you here?"

He glanced at the short line of customers. Charity was back from lunch break and handling the drinks, and Summer was fussing with the dog crate.

Bo walked up to Summer. "Would you mind keeping an eye on the dogs for Macy, just for a sec?" he asked.

Summer's eyes briefly met mine. I could read the look in them—she, too, could tell that Bo was acting anxious. "Sure, no prob."

With no explanation, Bo led me through the game area, where children were trying to win goldfish, stuffed animals, and any number of toys. We passed into a quieter area where Bo finally stopped, dropping his voice as he spoke.

"My old DEA boss just pulled me in on a special assignment. In recent years, they've suspected the fairground is a conduit for moving Fentanyl—a powerful synthetic opioid—but the DEA hasn't been able to determine which sector the drugs are passing through. This year, they've received a tip that the stables are where we need to look." He stopped and stared at me intensely. "I want you to stay well away from the horse area," he said. "Even though some of my DEA friends are posted nearby, these dealers are notoriously violent."

So *that* explained his sudden concern that I'd come from the stables.

"I understand," I said. I decided to be forthright with Bo. "Actually, I was trailing Tony Garten over there." I explained how I'd watched Tony fight with Reya before making a beeline for the stables. "I figured he was doing some illegal gambling and betting on the harness races, but do you think he's involved with the drug shipments somehow?"

"It's definitely not outside the realm of possibility. Since he's in the music industry, he'd have the right connections to know the drugs would be in town. I'll tell one of my guys to keep an eye on Tony if he shows up at the stables again."

"Thanks." I was glad Tony was going to come under more scrutiny, but I still wondered about Reya. What had gotten both her and Tony so worked up?

11

THE TWO DOGS that Summer had dropped off were a bit more antsy than usual, so I had to walk them often. One was an adorable puppy that looked like it had some Basset Hound in it. The pup kept trying to frisk around with the older dog, whose frisking days were long over. Walking seemed to be the best way to keep them separated. But the puppy was a big hit with children, and one boy even managed to talk his parents into adopting it.

I hoped the other dog would be adopted as well, but older dogs tended to go to older people, and since we were positioned near the kiddie ride area, we didn't see a lot of those, outside of grandparents who were raising their grandchildren, like Charity. I had such respect for those older family members who'd stepped up to the plate—it reminded me of Auntie A, who'd adopted us later in her life and was every bit a mother and a father rolled into one. We'd never noticed that she was the oldest "mom" at school activities, because she'd always *seemed* the same age as other moms.

I wrapped up my shift at four, when Milo came on board.

He both looked and smelled like a Tommy Hilfiger ad. I figured that wasn't an accident, since Bristol was due to arrive any moment to work at the booth with him.

Deciding against grabbing fair food for supper, I made my way to my car. As I got close, I noticed a couple standing near a blue hybrid car. The woman slouched against the door and wore a large, floppy hat, but I still easily recognized Carolina.

And the man who was about to pull her into a hug was Gage Hansen.

I ducked into my car before they could spot me. Was something going on between those two? I tried to peer out my window, but my view was blocked by the huge truck that had not-so-politely parked catty-corner next to me.

I started my car and inched it out, but by the time the blue car came into view, Carolina and Gage were already walking back toward the fairground.

Sure, it could've simply been a comforting hug—maybe because of Carolina's onstage shock. But what if it wasn't? What if those two were sneaking around on Tony? That changed the dynamic in their already-troubled relationship.

And what if Tony had already found out? Was he the jealous type who'd try to kill a wife who strayed? More likely, I was guessing he was the money-grubbing type who didn't want to lose his place in the band and his access to Carolina's money.

Either way, if Carolina and Gage *were* involved with each other, it provided another motivation for the attempts on her life, and she likely hadn't told Detective Hatcher about it.

Not to mention that if they were involved, Carolina had outright lied to me. She'd said Gage wasn't in a serious relationship and that he preferred to stay single. Had she been lying to me in other ways, as well? I couldn't help feeling a familiar sting of betrayal.

I didn't want to start acting all weird with Carolina, so it would probably be best to just up-front tell her I saw her with Gage and ask what was going on. But was that the best move? I needed some womanly input by someone older and wiser.

I knew just who to call.

Della Goddard, Bristol's mother, had been a listening ear to me before. She was widowed early, so we'd commiserated over our difficulties re-entering the dating world after marriage. I had come to trust her calmly spoken advice.

Once I got home and let Coal out, I sat down on my porch chair and gave Della a call. After some small talk about the Barks & Beans booth, I mentioned what I'd seen in the parking lot and asked if she thought it would be best to bring it up with Carolina. I knew Della was a veritable vault of secrecy and she wouldn't tell a soul what I'd shared with her.

As she often did, Della launched into a story to make a point. "My husband and I used to be close with another couple —we golfed with them, went out to eat with them, even celebrated our families' birthdays together. But one day I overheard her talking with another man on the phone, and I knew it wasn't her husband. I could tell she was deeply in love with this other man and probably having an affair with him. I wasn't sure what to do. If I told my husband, he would be grieved, and the burden would be on him to tell his best friend. I wrestled with whether I should approach anyone at all with what I'd discovered. Finally, I decided to go to my best friend and tell her I knew she was cheating, urging her to 'fess up' to her sweet, oblivious husband." Della suddenly fell silent.

I couldn't hide my impatience. "So? How did things go?"

Della cleared her throat. "Unfortunately, my friend refused to admit it, even though she knew I'd overheard their entire conversation. She cut off our friendship—and who knows how she explained *that* to her husband. Of course, Scott started asking me why our friends never wanted to get together anymore, so I had to tell him about my confrontation." Her voice caught, and I knew she was fighting back tears as she thought of her dead husband. "He told me I'd done exactly the right thing. He said if the woman had been a true friend, she would've listened to my warning and admitted the truth. And do you know what? The truth finally must've come out, because those friends divorced six months later."

I had to wonder if Scott had spoken to his friend in the interim, but that was neither here nor there. "Thank you so much, Della. You've helped me know just what to do."

I KNEW Carolina would return late from the concert, so I cobbled together a simple meal of stir-fry chicken and veggies. I returned to the porch to eat, wanting to enjoy the final flowers of the season.

A spunky shorter lady with gray hair walked up to my gate. Cupping her hands to her mouth, she shouted, "Yoo-hoo!"

Since Coal was inside, I set my plate on the chair and hurried over to greet her. "Hi, there."

She extended a hand. "Hi. I'm your new neighbor. My name's Vera Cox. And you must be Macy."

I wondered how she knew my name, but it was a smaller town. "Yes. I'm Macy Hatfield." I gestured toward my house. "As you probably knew, the Barks & Beans Cafe is attached to my place. My brother and I run it."

She gave a delighted bob of her head. "Oh, yes. I can't wait to visit it—probably when I get everything unpacked and feel a little less helter-skelter, you know? A place for everything and everything in its place, you understand." She peered through her nineties-style bifocals at me. "I knew your aunt Athaleen," she said unexpectedly.

"Oh, you did?" I looked at her. She was at least ten years younger than Auntie A, I was sure. "Have I met you before?"

"Oh, no—we became friends after you'd moved away from home, I believe. Then I moved soon after. But law, *law*...the adventures we had!"

My interest was piqued. Detective Hatcher had also alluded to some kind of adventures my great aunt had gotten into.

Coal gave a gigantic bark from inside the house. "I have a Great Dane," I explained. "I'm sorry, but I probably need to go check on him. It's been great meeting you, Vera. Let's get together sometime when you get all unpacked."

Vera, who was shorter than me by a couple of inches, smiled. "I'd love to meet your dog sometime." She waved and walked toward her house.

I grabbed my plate and hurried inside to see what Coal was riled up about, since he rarely barked at nothing. But this was one of those exceptions to the rule. He was staring at a wasp that had somehow made its way into the house. The wasp banged against the window, trying to get out. Coal was licking his lips as if ready to eat the pesky insect.

"Nope, you don't want that," I said, grabbing my flyswatter.

Coal tried to edge around me to get first dibs, but I batted the wasp down before snatching it up with a tissue. Coal trailed me into the bathroom as I flushed it down the toilet. "Thanks for letting me know about it, boy."

His tail wagged, thudding into the cabinet. That sturdy tail had bruised my legs several times, so I steered him out of the room before he had time to damage anything in the small space.

We settled into the couch to watch TV. Time seemed to fly by and the next thing I knew, the lock was turning on my back door. I glanced at my phone to see it was already 10:32. I knew it had to be Bo or Carolina, since I'd given her my extra key.

Sure enough, Carolina came in, looking pretty wiped out. She kicked her heels off and headed for a chair.

I stood. "Have you eaten? You look pooped."

She nodded. "I am pooped, but yes, I grabbed a piece of pizza after the concert."

"How'd it go?" I asked, flipping on another light.

"We closed the show out a little early, and do you want to know why? Because Reya never showed up. I had to do a couple of songs without her—high parts—and I'm sure they sounded awful."

My mind flew to the argument I'd witnessed earlier. I didn't want to hit my exhausted friend with even more bad news about her husband, but I felt I had no other choice.

"Good grief, I'm sorry to hear that. Do you want some tea or hot chocolate?" I offered, trying to smooth the way for what I needed to tell her.

"Sure, hot chocolate would be perfect." She managed a grin. "Do you happen to have any of those mini marshmallows we used to gorge ourselves on?"

I laughed. "You know, I think Auntie A left some in her cabinet. They might not be expired yet." After rummaging around, I found a bag of heart-shaped mini marshmallows and held it up triumphantly.

"Thanks." She propped her feet on the ottoman and rested her head on the chair.

Setting the teakettle on to boil, I said, "Listen...about Reya. I saw her today."

"Oh, yeah? I saw her, too. She was at the Crush Bus in the morning. But where'd you see her?"

I pulled out a cobalt blue Barks & Beans Cafe mug. Bristol had helped with the design and I'd ordered myself several colors. After scooping hot chocolate mix into it, I said, "Reya was arguing with Tony."

"What?" She sat up straighter. "Where was this?"

Leaning on the counter to face her, I said, "It was near the Bingo tent. They didn't think anyone could see them, but I was up in the Ferris wheel."

"What were they arguing about?" she demanded.

"I have no idea. They were definitely shouting. I saw him grab her arms, too." I grabbed the kettle just before it whistled. After mixing up the hot chocolate, I sprinkled a liberal helping of marshmallows on top.

Carolina glowered. "Great. *Just* great. What's he up to now?"

I walked the hot chocolate over to her and placed it on a coaster. "Be careful, it's super hot." As I sat down on the couch, I gently said, "I saw something else today."

She quirked an eyebrow, waiting for me to elaborate.

"Carolina, I saw you and Gage in the parking lot. Now, I know that might not mean anything—"

She gave a long blink and frowned. "No, you're right. I should come clean. I don't know why I tried to hide it from you. Gage...he's been so close to me all these years. Then, just last year, something shifted, and it was like we became aware of each other on a romantic level. We tried to skirt the issue every time we were alone together, but our feelings kind of took over."

While I appreciated her acknowledgment of the truth and I knew Tony was a jerk, I still had a hard time stomaching that Carolina was a cheater.

"Gage just listened to me," she explained, probably reading the look on my face. "Unlike Tony, he wanted what was best for the band, not just for himself."

Before I had a chance to respond, her phone pinged. She picked it up and read the text. Her face blanched. "Reya's not at the hotel. Murphy and Tony checked her room. Why would she skip the concert and stay out so long?"

I took a deep breath, my mind stuck on another track. "Did Tony know about you and Gage?"

She gave a vigorous shake of her head. "No, we were very careful. Besides, Tony's out all the time."

I wasn't so sure. "There's still a possibility someone saw you and Gage and told him about it. Maybe Tony's the one who's been trying to kill you."

Tucking her feet beneath her, she took a tiny sip of hot chocolate. "No. I don't think he'd do that. He needs me too much."

"But we already know he can be violent, like he was with Reya today. I'm going to have to let Detective Hatcher know about their fight. And *you* need to tell him about you and Gage, since that could be some kind of motive for your attacks. Maybe this all ties together with Reya's disappearance, too."

Concern swept across her features. "Of course. I should've told him at the start. It was so stupid of me, but I couldn't believe anyone would try to kill me. I kept thinking the shock was a fluke and the Digoxin was some kind of weird accident." She uncurled and stretched her legs. "Oh. I forgot something else. Guess who was at the concert tonight, and right up front? Aidan Conley. I didn't see Mattie with him, either."

Alarm shot through me. "With all that's been going on, maybe he needs to be added to the person of interest list as someone who might try to harm you. I mean, maybe Mattie just didn't feel like coming to another concert she didn't care for, but doesn't it seem creepy that Aidan would pay for a second concert ticket and leave his wife at home? Given what Sheldia said about his preoccupation with the band, maybe we'd better give Detective Hatcher a call."

12

AFTER FILLING the detective in on Tony and Aidan, we stayed up, hoping to hear some good news about Reya. Carolina texted Murphy, asking him to tell her immediately if Reya showed up, but she said he wasn't much help. At this stage, he was acting like his nerves were shot. I had to say I felt for him—having to deal with the media about Carolina's near-death experiences, rearrange the concert schedule, and handle a band member's sudden disappearance were heavy responsibilities, even for a band manager.

To keep ourselves awake, we flipped through the photo albums Auntie A had thoughtfully put together over the years. Finding one with plenty of photos of the two of us, we took turns squealing over our fashion choices back in the day. We actually found a school trip photo with Mattie in the shot—and I was sure it was the only photo of Mattie in my entire house.

Carolina pressed her finger to the photo, blocking out Mattie's face. "You know, she really was a scourge on our class," she said. "Remember that crush I had on Randy Mack? She went and swooped him out from under me."

I laughed. "I don't think you ever 'had' Randy to begin with. I think he was into *me*."

Coal gave an impressive yawn from his pillow, thus letting us know it was way past his bedtime and he wasn't situated in the proper room yet.

"Sorry, boy." I stood and stretched toward the ceiling. "We'd better hit the sack. You were wiped out when you got back. I'm thinking they won't find Reya tonight. Hopefully she'll show up tomorrow."

"She has to," Carolina said. "The Crush Bus leaves tomorrow night. Our driver has to get back for his son's wedding." She stood, lean and leggy as a cheetah. "Do you care if I stay on another night, though? I planned to rent a car and drive the scenic route home."

"Of course. You know my door is always open for you, Carolina."

She gave me a quick hug and walked off to her room. I let Coal out one more time before bed. He nearly scared the flip flops off me when he first rumbled, then exploded with one thunderous bark. My dog, who had a serious phobia of my garden shed, now charged straight toward it. I stood with my mouth open, vaguely wondering when an adult would deal with him, but I quickly realized that adult was supposed to be *me*.

"Get back here," I hissed, wishing the old solar lights lining the pathway were brighter. Several bulbs had been knocked out by Coal's tail, so there were large patches of darkness.

He came panting up toward me. At least he'd only allowed himself one horrifying bark at this late hour. He'd obviously been chasing something, but what? Deer rarely jumped my fence to browse along my flowerbeds, but it did happen. Maybe tonight was one of those nights. While Coal might bark at wasps while stuck inside, when he was *outside* the house, he ignored all animals smaller than raccoons or skunks.

I hoped he hadn't gotten the wind up on a skunk. He'd had a run-in with one when he'd first arrived, and given how pitifully he'd whined when I'd washed him down with a baking soda concoction afterward, I'd assumed he'd never try it again.

"C'mon inside," I breathed, tugging at his collar. "This isn't the time for a wild goose chase."

I locked the door as soon as we were in, then led Coal straight up to the bedroom. Maybe he was just overtired and seeing things. But for him to go charging toward the dreaded garden shed, I had to admit the possibility that he'd perceived some kind of danger.

And I wondered if it was the human kind.

Tuesday morning dawned with the type of murky gray skies that indicated rain might be on the way. Although our iced coffee booth was covered, our employees moved around a lot and would likely still get wet. It was my day off, but I'd agreed to help Bo and Kylie open the stand just to get things moving faster.

Coal was dragging around and Carolina was still asleep when I poured my hot tea into a travel mug and headed out around seven. It was the kind of day that made me want to stay inside and reread a classic like *The Count of Monte Cristo.* As if the ominous skies weren't enough, I still felt uneasy about Reya.

Bo was already ahead of things when I arrived. Giving me a hug, he asked, "Did you sleep well?"

Before I could answer, Kylie jogged over, out of breath. She looked more put-together today, so I hoped she'd had a better night's sleep.

"Something's happened on the grounds," she said. "I came in by the grandstand, and the place was crawling with cops. And get this—behind their police tape, I watched them take someone out on a stretcher—in a body bag. They're trying to keep people away, but a crowd is building over by the bleachers."

My stomach dropped. I had a strong guess as to whose body they'd discovered. "Bo, could you call Detective Hatcher and ask if they've found Reya?"

"You mean Reya Heres from Carolina Crush?" Kylie's eyes were wide.

I put a finger to my lips. "Let's keep things quiet until we know for sure."

She nodded and began to set out cups.

Bo did as I asked and called the detective. His serious look only deepened as he listened for a while. When he hung up, he took me aside and dropped his voice. "Sis, I hate to tell you, but it was Reya. They'd searched the stage area last night and came up empty, but this morning, one of the stage crew noticed flies buzzing around a metal panel on the floor. He said it's looking like someone coshed her over the head with something heavy and dumped her."

I tried to contain my disgust that someone would kill Reya and drop her like a sack of potatoes in some kind of hole under the stage. "It has to be someone familiar with the stage layout," I mused. "Has anyone called the band manager or Carolina?"

Bo said that Murphy had been informed, but the detective hadn't mentioned Carolina. Compelled to check in on my friend, I begged off and headed straight home.

I fumbled with the lock and came in to find Carolina crying on the living room floor. Coal was sitting close to her.

I rushed to her side. "You heard?"

"Mm-hm," she said, her voice muffled. Her face was red and puffy as she turned to me. "Who would *do* such a thing to her?" she wailed. "I'll never find a better backup singer. She was so instinctive."

I rubbed her back, knowing she was in shock. "I know, I know. I'm sure Detective Hatcher will find out who did this."

She shook her head miserably. "I doubt it. He hasn't even figured out who was trying to kill me—and now I'm convinced that someone was definitely trying to do that. The detective told me they found an extension cord from the stage that had its ground pin cut. Although I've heard of people doing that to cut humming in the sound system, it definitely seems malicious to me."

I nodded. "And now it's looking like they weren't just targeting you, but *all* the band members. Have you talked to Tony or Gage?"

"I texted them. They were planning to leave with the bus tonight, but the detective asked everyone to stay longer while he's checking into things. He asked me to stick around, too. You sure you don't mind if I stay on?"

"Of course. You'll be safe here at my place."

"I know." She sniffled and patted Coal's head. "He's a good guard dog."

I recalled his barking episode last night. Had someone come to our house, then given up and targeted Reya instead? I didn't think a single dog bark was worth telling the detective about, but I'd have to keep a sharp eye on things, just in case.

After fixing a breakfast of eggs and toast for us, I did some loads of laundry. Around eleven, Jimmy texted me from the cafe, saying he was sneezing and starting to feel like he was catching a cold. I told him to go home and that I would fill in at the Barks section for the rest of the day.

Tiptoeing to Carolina's closed door, I tapped on it and asked if she was okay if I headed to the cafe for a while. "I won't be far away," I assured her.

She opened the door. She was dressed for the day and had made the effort to put on makeup. "That's fine, Macy. I'll be signing for a rental car soon—they're driving it over to me."

That was unusual, but I supposed the rental car place was happy to deliver a car to a star like her. I gave Carolina a hug and headed for the cafe.

The familiar smells were comforting as I stepped in. I walked over and commiserated with Jimmy a little before he left, then I whipped myself up a cafe mocha before I settled in with the dogs. The older dog from yesterday was now hanging out in the Barks section, and another mid-sized dog was going from one toy to another, enjoying his newly spacious digs.

I had just taken a sip of my mocha when a familiar voice sounded above the low brick divider wall. "Hello, Macy."

I looked up to see Dylan, who was looking all country club in his zip-up, coffee-colored shirt and straight leg white jeans. His dark blue eyes were fixed on me.

"Hi, Dylan." I set my coffee on a nearby table and stood to greet him. "How's business?"

We talked about our work for a while, then our conversation took a surprising turn.

Dylan gave me a concerned look. "The news said that someone was found dead at the fair. Police haven't released any details, but one of my employees said the fan pages are buzzing that it was one of the Carolina Crush band members. Do you know if that's true?"

Had he put two and two together and realized that the woman I'd brought into his gallery the other day was Carolina Garten, country superstar? It was possible, especially if one of his employees had spotted her.

I wasn't sure how much information I was allowed to share. "I can't say much, but if you're worried about Carolina, my friend who visited your gallery the other day, she's okay."

He nodded. "I was. I'm sorry I didn't recognize her immediately. I felt bad when Shanda told me who she was."

I grinned. "I think Carolina found your lack of recognition refreshing." Was he interested in her? I wasn't sure how to feel about that.

"You know me—I avoid popular music. By the way, they're doing a concert Friday night at Carnegie Hall—would you want to join me? We could grab something to eat afterward."

Okay, so obviously Dylan *was* still into me. I didn't want to lead him on, but was it really leading him on when I was simply harboring interest in another guy who had never even asked me out? After all, Dylan and I were already pretty close friends. It couldn't hurt to hang out with him more, but maybe I should establish some kind of ground rules, so he didn't get his hopes up.

His eyes traced over my face, as if he were trying to read my every thought.

"Uh, sure. I always have a good time with you." Wait, that didn't sound like ground rules.

"Good." He gave me an excited smile. "Just text me where you'd like to eat."

After we said our goodbyes and he headed out, I took a slow sip of my too-cool mocha. Sometime, I was going to have to sit down and work through my feelings for Dylan Butler and my *other* feelings for Titan McCoy and come to some kind of definitive conclusion.

Looking out at the overcast skies, I sighed. That day was not today.

13

AFTER CLOSING THE CAFE, I headed out on the sidewalk to get some fresh air on my way home. After the lightest drizzle of rain, the gray clouds had cleared, leaving behind blue skies.

As I unlatched my back gate, Vera gave a shout from her front porch.

I peered between her shaggy hedges, only to see her hurrying my way, a glass of iced sweet tea clinking in her hand.

"Macy!" She opened her white picket gate and came to my side. Her breath caught before she spoke. "I need to tell you something." She jabbed her finger toward my flower garden. "Along about fifteen minutes ago, a man walked up the sidewalk by your house. Now that wasn't strange in and of itself, but he kept lingering by your fence. Then, all of a sudden, he opened your gate and went into your garden. Straight in! I wasn't sure if you might be expecting someone, so I didn't feel right checking up on him."

Her large brown eyes, somehow reminiscent of one my favorite dogs of childhood, looked up at me imploringly.

Nervousness shot through me. "No, I wasn't expecting

anyone." Unsure if I should call Bo or even the police, I leaned over the gate and looked into my garden. Most of the nooks and crannies were exposed in the daylight, and I couldn't see anyone hiding there. Maybe the man had gotten the wrong house.

I turned back to Vera, confused. "Did he come back out again?"

She frowned. "I wasn't sure. See, the mailman came right after that, so I walked over to get my mail. He might've left then."

I nodded. "Okay, do you mind standing here a second? I'm going to let my dog out."

As if suddenly realizing she was still holding onto her glass, she carefully set it on the ground next to the fence. Glancing around, she grabbed a long stick that had fallen onto the sidewalk and held it up like a baseball bat. "Sure. I'm ready."

I grinned at the older woman's pluck. After opening my gate, I raced for the front door, shoved my key in, and opened it. Coal burst out in all his glory, as if he knew exactly what his task was. Pushing right by me, he plowed straight into the garden, sniffing everything. He hesitated at the shed, but only for a second. After using the bathroom and making the loop, he trotted right back to my side.

I gave a thumbs-up to Vera. "I think it's okay. He'd let me know if someone were still here. The guy must've had the wrong place and headed back out when you weren't looking."

She leaned over her fence and dropped the stick in her yard, probably planning to deal with it later when she cleared up the overgrown landscaping. "Okay, then." She took a step toward my fence. "And this is your beautiful dog?"

Realizing I hadn't properly introduced her, I walked Coal over. "This is my big boy, Coal." He politely sat down and let the small woman pat his head.

She seemed to be in awe. "I've never seen a dog this tall before."

"It's kind of hard to comprehend how big Great Danes are until you see one up close," I said with a nod of agreement. It was getting late, and with Carolina staying with me, I needed to figure out a supper plan. I gave a parting wave to Vera. "Thank you again. I'd better get back in for now."

"Of course. We'll talk later, I'm sure." She walked toward her place, her steps spritely. She seemed to have more energy than I did at thirty-eight.

Coal walked ahead of me into the house. "Carolina?" I called out, but there was no reply. I knocked on the guest room door, but she still didn't answer. Assuming she was either taking a nap or that she'd gone out in her new rental car, I decided to go ahead and order Chinese food.

I was fairly certain that Carolina favored orange chicken when we were younger, so I took a chance and ordered some, along with plenty of lo mein, fried rice, and dumplings.

I had just poured myself some water when the doorbell rang. Coal gave three loud barks, running toward it.

"Hang on, hang on," I muttered. Just in case some weirdo *had* been lurking around my garden, I slid open the drawer in my side table and grabbed my pepper spray. Not that I'd really need it with Coal blocking the doorway.

I opened the door and was dumbfounded to see Tony Garten standing there. His dark, hipster beard was looking rough around the edges, like he hadn't trimmed it in a while, and his eyes were bloodshot.

Coal backed up, literally shoving me backward, and gave a huge warning *woof*.

I placed a hand on Coal's shoulder. "He's not great with strangers," I said. There was no way I was going to welcome Tony into my home.

He didn't pay attention to my unsociable vibes. Desperation charged his voice. "Is Carolina here?"

She must've told him she was staying with me, but I really wished she hadn't. "I'm not sure—what do you need?"

"I need to talk with her. Right away," he demanded.

Somewhat affronted, I stood my ground. "I don't think she's here."

"Could you go check for me?" He kept moving, shifting from one foot to another, like a little boy anxious to get to the bathroom.

That was it. I wasn't bringing Carolina out to meet this joker. "No, I couldn't and I won't. Now, I suggest you get going and leave my friend alone."

He gave a callous laugh. "Your *friend*? That woman doesn't know how to be a friend." He slapped the doorframe, his volume getting louder. "You tell her to call me the minute you see her again. She's not getting away with this." His reddened eyes stared past me, into the house. "You hear me? *You can't do this to me!*" he shouted as if Carolina could hear him.

The moment he raised his voice, Coal tried to charge him, but I grabbed his collar and held him back. I could see Vera standing on the sidewalk. She was holding up her portable phone and pointing to it, obviously asking if I wanted her to call the cops.

I gave a brief shake of my head. Tony was upset, all right, but I didn't think he meant to do me harm. It was Carolina he wanted to see for some dark reason.

"Get going, Tony," I said firmly. "Don't do something stupid. My dog probably weighs more than you, and he's not letting you take one step into this house. I'll tell Carolina you stopped by. Now, *get*."

The slim man stumbled backward and down the steps, muttering to himself the whole way. He slammed through the gate, took one look at Vera, who stood by her fence looking fierce, and jogged off across the street.

I waved. "Thanks, Vera. I'm going to let the police know about this. We're okay."

She nodded. "I figured you had it under control, but I wanted to be here, just in case."

As she walked away, I didn't know if I should feel grateful or annoyed. I certainly understood that some people were just born to be protective—like my brother Bo—so I decided not to get annoyed that Vera seemed to have injected herself into my single-girl life. Tony had seemed highly unstable, so there was no telling what he might've done next if he hadn't heeded my warnings.

Heading back inside, I rapped on Carolina's door again, but there was no answer. She really should know that her husband was running around demanding to see her. I hesitantly pushed her door open and looked around. Her bed was made and her room had been tidied up. She was nowhere in sight.

Pulling my phone from my pocket, I shot her a text letting her know Tony was upset and looking for her. I told her I'd ordered Chinese for supper if she wanted to eat here.

I didn't want to jump to conclusions that Carolina had disappeared like Reya had. Most likely, she'd taken her rental car to run an errand in town.

The Chinese food was delivered, and I had just served myself a portion of the steaming rice when there was a short knock on the door. "Sis?" Bo's welcome voice sounded outside.

Coal padded over to greet my brother as I opened the door for him. "Come in and have some Chinese," I said.

"That's okay," he said. "I'm out on my jog, but I wanted to stop in and see how things went at the cafe."

I caught him up on the day, telling him about the man ducking into my garden and about Tony's unwelcome drop-in visit. Bo didn't waste time going straight outside to double-check that the garden was clear. When he rejoined me at the table, he looked serious.

"You think Carolina's okay?" he asked.

"I don't know for sure," I admitted.

"I should call—"

The doorbell rang again and Coal barked. My house certainly was a popular place tonight.

Bo strode over and opened the door. Coal edged over by his side.

You could've knocked me over with a twig when I realized it was Mattie Bully-Pants Conley standing there. Jumping to my feet and walking toward Bo, I instructed Coal to sit. I felt conflicted when I realized Mattie was carrying a tiny baby in the sling across her chest.

To my complete surprise, she was downright apologetic. "Hi, guys. I'm sorry to bother y'all. Macy, I looked for your number online but couldn't find it, so I figured I'd drop by." She patted at the baby's back with her chipped green nails as she bounced in place. "I know this is strange, but I'm looking for my husband, Aidan."

I was instantly on the alert. "Why would he be here?"

Her sheepish look only intensified, making her look like a completely different person than the kid who'd loved to make others suffer. "I called over to his job—he's with J & D Construction—and they said he never showed up this morning. But I heard him leave early."

"So you're wondering where he is," Bo said. "Why would you assume he was here, though?"

I already knew the answer to that question, but Mattie went on to explain.

"To be honest, he's been totally distracted ever since Carolina Garten came back to town. I knew he was a big fan of

Carolina Crush—he has all kinds of signed posters and things in the basement. But lately, he's been going out at all hours. Last night, I decided to check his phone while he was in the bathroom, and I found lots of pictures of Carolina at the fairground. They weren't taken at the concert. They were zoomed-up photos of her near the tour bus, walking around in a hat, things like that." Mattie's lips wavered.

"He's stalking her," I said, my suspicions about Aidan validated.

Bo nodded. "I'll call my friend Detective Hatcher and let him know what you said. He's the lead detective working on the death of the band member, Reya."

An actual tear dropped from Mattie's eye and plopped onto her baby's light hair. "Oh, I'm sure he had nothing to do with that," she said. "I just knew she was staying with you because...well, because he mentioned it one night at supper. I wanted to check and see if he was here, that's all."

"He hasn't been here that I know of," I said, unable to believe I was trying to help our old enemy. "We'll talk with the detective, and I'll text Carolina and let her know to watch out for Aidan."

"I'm sure he wouldn't hurt her," Mattie babbled on. "He just loves the band, that's all."

I could tell she was trying to talk herself into believing that. "Why don't you take your baby home now," I suggested, rubbing between Coal's ears. "We'll make sure the right people know about this. You try not to worry."

"Okay, sure." Her uneasy look belied her casual words. "Thank you." She turned and carefully headed down the stairs, her hand on her child. Who would've thought the bully of the century would turn out to be a caring mother? Before she made it to the gate, she turned. "Oh, and here's my number." She recited it, and in a surreal moment, I entered my old enemy's cell number in my phone.

When she got out of earshot, I said, "Bo, that makes two men who are out hunting for Carolina. We have to get to her first and warn her. I'd go out looking for her, but I don't even know what kind of rental car they gave her."

"Probably a nice one," Bo mused, "But that's nothing new in this town. No—you sit tight here and let me know if she shows up. I'm going to talk with Charlie about Tony's visit and tell him what Mattie said about Aidan. He can probably have someone tail those guys."

"Okay," I said, wishing I could do more.

As Bo jogged out toward his house, I went inside and locked the door behind me. I couldn't be too careful, and hopefully Carolina was watching her step, too—wherever she was.

14

Darkness fell, and I let Coal sprawl on the couch next to me. He kept my feet warm in the air conditioning, plus I felt safer with him so close by.

The key twisted in the lock and we were both instantly alert, waiting to see who came in.

Carolina walked in and took her shoes off by the door. "Hey, girl."

I jumped up. "Hey, yourself! Why didn't you answer any of my texts or calls?"

"What are you talking about?" She yanked her phone from the side pocket of her leather satchel and thumbed at the screen. "Oh, shoot...I see all your messages now. I was out of cell range for half my trip, so I just let the calls and texts go until I got back. I'm sorry. What's going on?"

"You're going to want to sit down for this. Did you eat? And where *were* you, by the way?"

She sat down at the table. "No, I haven't eaten yet. And I was out driving the backroads. Country roads, take me home and all that." She offered a wan smile. "I needed to get away from everything and really think about what's going on...try to process the seriousness of it, you know?" She leaned forward. "Do you have food?"

"I sure do. I ordered Chinese—orange chicken still your fave?"

"You remembered! Sounds delicious. Thank you."

I grabbed the cartons and scooped food onto a plate. "I'm going to begin at the beginning." I shared about the man Vera saw, about Tony's irate visit, and finally, about Mattie's search for her husband.

"Carolina, I'm telling you, I've never seen Mattie so vulnerable in my entire life," I said, popping the plate in the microwave.

Carolina nodded. "I'll bet. I mean, she must love him to be willing to book tickets to come to our concert—all the while knowing how obsessed he was with the band."

"Correction: with *you*." I handed her the plate and a fork. "Carolina, it's safe to say he's obsessed with you. Have you ever had any stalker fans before?"

She shrugged. "It's kind of par for the course. I don't think Aidan's any worse than any others. That's why we hire security when we go to shows."

"But some fans get much more personal than others," I persisted. "Showing up at stars' homes, sending death threats, and all that."

She picked at her lo mein, taking the onions out of it. "Trust me, I get it. But again, I'm not too worried about Aidan. He's a married man with kids who just happens to have a crush on me."

I felt Carolina was blowing the whole thing off way too easily, but that was how she'd approached every dangerous run-in she'd had on this trip. If I were her, I'd hire my own bodyguards and hide somewhere Aidan could never find me.

Actually, come to think of it, I wouldn't have to hire any bodyguards—I'd have Bo. He was better than an entire army when he geared up to protect his little sister. It was too bad Carolina's younger brother Claude wasn't more like mine.

I wasn't ready to give up. "What about when you were out driving around...did you stop anywhere or see anyone suspicious?"

She got a water bottle and unscrewed the cap. "I don't think so. I didn't get out anywhere since the rental had a full tank of gas." After taking a drink, she stopped. "Well, there was this red truck behind me on the way back. It was kind of annoying, because he kept getting close, but he wouldn't pass in the passing zones. I figured he was one of those erratic older drivers that have bad vision or something."

I pushed for more information. "What did the truck look like?"

"It was definitely old," she said. "It had this loud muffler."

"And it followed you all the way home?"

"No, it pulled off somewhere in town, which is why I didn't think it was following me."

"Hang on," I said. After sucking in a deep breath, I grabbed my phone, scrolled down to Mattie's number, and called her.

"Hello?" She sounded distracted.

"Mattie, it's Macy Hatfield." I didn't know why I said my last name—there were no other Macys around. "I won't keep you long. Does Aidan have a truck?"

"Mm-hm," she said. "A red one. It's an old Dodge Ram. Why?"

"Is he home yet?"

"No, and he hasn't called, either. Did you find him?" She sounded a little more scared than hopeful.

"Not exactly. I'm just checking up on something. I'm sure the detective will call you if he finds him." Hanging up, I looked at Carolina. "I'm nearly a hundred percent sure that was Aidan following you."

She paled. "Did he follow me here?"

"I don't know," I said. "I'm calling Bo."

Bo DIDN'T WASTE any time warning Detective Hatcher to keep an eye out for the red Dodge truck. Then he asked me to call Mattie and talk her into staying with her parents, who lived a couple of counties over, for the night. When I tried to protest, he immediately shut me down.

"Sis, I've read up on plenty of stalker cases and even worked with someone who protected stars for a living," Bo said. "It can turn ugly in a heartbeat, and there's even a possibility that Aidan could return home and do something awful to his family in order to be left alone in his single-minded pursuit of Carolina. In other words, I'm not asking you, I'm *telling* you to convince Mattie to get those kids out of there now. Otherwise, I'll have to go over and do it, and I'm not nearly as nice as you."

He didn't have to say another word. "Consider it done," I said.

It didn't take long for Mattie to agree with the plan. She promised to call her parents the moment she hung up with me and stay at their place until someone found Aidan.

Meanwhile, Carolina had gone into her room to call the other loose cannon, Tony. I wondered what he needed to say that was so terribly important he had to show up at my house and be belligerent in front of my intimidating dog. Most people would've backed down at Coal's first bark.

Uncertain what the next step was in keeping Carolina safe, I gave Bo another call.

With no preamble, he said, "I'm staying at your place tonight."

"Okay." Goosebumps went up my arms. My brother would never suggest such a thing unless he genuinely thought we weren't safe—even with Coal around.

"I'll be over soon. Don't worry, I'll let myself in so you can go on to bed. Coal can stay upstairs with you, and I'll sleep on the couch. You can just let Carolina know I'll be staying over so she won't freak out if she sees a dude on the couch in the middle of the night."

"You got it." This was one of those times when Bo commanded and I simply fell into line because I was smart enough to recognize that he'd chosen the best plan of action.

I hung up and knocked on Carolina's door.

"Come in," she said.

She was lying on the bed in her pajamas, her eyes red like she'd been crying.

"Did you get a hold of Tony?" I asked.

She nodded. "He wants me to come back...says he can't live without me. He said we can drive the rental car and take our time heading back to Nashville, do a regular road trip together."

I felt pressure behind my eyes, like a headache was building. "Did he also say he's going to stop gambling?"

She scooted to the edge of the bed and grabbed a tissue. After blowing her nose, she said, "No, he didn't, and I'm not a fool. Of course I'm not going with him. In fact, I've decided to fly home as soon as the detective gives us the all-clear to go."

"Has he been questioning the band about Reya, do you know?"

She nodded. "Just Tony, so far—he brought him down to the station today. I think that's part of why Tony's so freaked out. Maybe the detective brought up his massive debt or something."

"I'm just glad you're keeping your head screwed on straight," I said. "I wouldn't trust Tony at this point if I were you."

"No way." She propped herself up on a couple of pillows.

"Listen," I said. "I came in to tell you that Bo's sleeping on my couch tonight. He wants to be an extra line of defense, just in case Aidan tries to sneak in or something."

Carolina raised an eyebrow. "Your skinny ginger brother's coming over to try to protect me?" She snickered.

For the first time in a long time, I felt upset with her. "Don't mock my brother," I said. "You haven't seen him in years." Of course, she had no idea that Bo had been in the DEA—he'd only just told me about that last year.

"I can't imagine he's changed that much." Her tone was condescending.

I stood, irritated by her attitude. "I wanted to let you know so you wouldn't get scared in the night, that's all. I'm heading to bed."

She didn't even apologize as I walked out and rejoined Coal in the hallway. I made sure all the doors were locked and traipsed upstairs.

Carolina might have convinced herself she was untouchable, but that was just an illusion. Someone had tried to kill her twice, and now it was clear that Aidan was stalking her. She needed to get her head in the game.

I was on edge as I put on my PJs and slipped under the quilt. Coal circled on his pillow and was about to doze off when he raised his head, listening.

Faintly, I could hear the back door opening and I knew it was Bo. I didn't feel like extracting myself from bed to go down and say goodnight. Thankfully, Bo saved me the trouble of getting up, texting that he was on the couch and all the doors were locked. I knew what he'd left unsaid—that he was armed and ready if someone tried to get in downstairs.

Coal seemed to recognize that it was Bo—whether he could smell him that far away or was simply so familiar with his ways, I didn't know—and he sank back onto his pillow.

I closed my eyes, resting in the certainty that my place was well-guarded by both man and beast. I had to shut out the memory of Carolina's snide comments about Bo. At the very least, she could show a little more gratitude for our attempts to bring her under our sheltering wing while she was in Lewisburg. After all, we Hatfields could be a formidable bunch.

15

MORNING LIGHT STREAMED through my blinds as I woke to the smells of ham and eggs. Bless my brother's heart, he was making breakfast for us. I took a quick shower, dressed, and threw on a little makeup before heading downstairs.

Carolina was up early, sitting on the couch and openly staring at Bo, who was turned toward the frying pan. He wore a dark gray tank top that showed off his Marine tattoos and his muscles. I could tell from the dazzled look on her face that she hadn't counted on my "skinny ginger brother" growing up to become such a specimen of masculinity. I had to hide my smile.

"Good morning, all," I sang out.

Carolina gave a half turn toward me. "I was just sitting here catching up with Bo. He seems to know all there is to know about coffee beans."

I couldn't tell if she was subtly saying Bo was nerdy or if she was genuinely impressed with the extent of his knowledge. Regardless, she was obviously dazzled with his looks, given that she'd already returned to watching him cook.

"Yes, he's the coffee genius who masterminded the Barks & Beans Cafe. Stepping into that business was a lifesaver for me."

She nodded. "Macy, we still haven't gotten a chance to talk about your divorce."

"Trust me, you're not missing out on much." I walked over and threw a coffee pod in the coffeemaker. There was no time for fancying things up with my French press today. Bo and I needed to get to the fairgrounds. But where would that leave Carolina?

"What're you up to today?" I asked her, taking the full plate Bo handed me. Carolina sprang to her feet to get her plate—touching Bo's hand as she did so.

I supposed she was used to men falling at her feet, but she didn't know my brother. It took him a while to get interested in someone, and when he did, he literally had eyes for no one else. Right now, I was pretty sure Summer had taken up all his romantic headspace. He sat down at the table, bowed his head briefly, and started eating.

Carolina hurried to join him at the table. "I don't know, Macy. I feel like staying alone here might be dangerous. Are you two going to work at the fair or the cafe today?"

"The fair," Bo answered, taking a swig of orange juice. "We're both on duty today."

She nodded. "I think I'll pack up and go over there, too."

Trying to dispel any notions she might have of shadowing Bo at our booth, I said, "I guess you'll be hanging out in the Crush Bus. It's great that you all have air conditioning in it."

"Right," she said, her voice unsure. "Although I don't want to be trapped with Tony for any length of time."

"Her husband," I deliberately explained to Bo, although he was fully aware of that fact.

Bo's amused blue eyes met my own. I could tell that he was

both aware of Carolina's interest in him and of my annoyance with it.

He stood and rinsed his plate in the sink. "I'd better get home and jump in the shower. I'll see you at the fair, Macy." He nodded at Carolina. "Good to see you. Take care."

Shoving his feet into his tennis shoes, he jogged out the door.

Carolina let out a huge gush of breath. "Holy cow, Macy. Why didn't you ever tell me your brother was such a massive hunk? He looks like a Viking."

I frowned. "Probably because you're *married*."

She tossed her head. "I won't be for long. I've decided to divorce Tony. He can take his own stupid road trips—alone. Plus, he can deal with his own debts. I plan to fly back to Nashville tomorrow, if Detective Hatcher gives me the okay. I'm going to use my money to move someplace a little more modest."

Hopefully, she wouldn't announce her plans to the world at large. If Tony *had* been the one to make attempts on Carolina's life in order to hold onto the bulk of her estate, he'd only accelerate his attempts if he found out she planned to divorce him, leaving him nothing.

"Don't tell Tony that, at least until you get home and move away from him," I urged.

"We'll see," she said carelessly. "I can't pretend that I still want to be married to him."

My voice hardened. "And what *do* you want, Carolina?"

She gave me a startled look. "I guess I hadn't really thought about it before."

Taking her plate and my own, I walked over to the sink. Thinking of her casual flirtation with Bo and her secret romance with Gage, I said, "Maybe it's time that you did."

CAROLINA RODE over with me to the fair. I'd managed to squelch some of my disappointment with her two-timing ways by reminding myself that she'd been the recent victim of a couple of near-death experiences, which was bound to throw anyone for a loop.

After we parked, I walked her across the dewy grass to the Crush Bus, where Murphy welcomed us into the kitchenette. Sipping at a mug of coffee, he asked us to sit down for a moment.

"Tony and Gage are in the back, working on some new songs," he said. "And Detective Hatcher came by. He said Reya was killed on Monday night, and not on Tuesday morning when they found her. They're checking into everyone's whereabouts that night, and they've already talked with Tony about some argument he'd had with Reya." He absently rubbed at his bald spot. "I hadn't heard about an argument, and Tony's not sharing anything with me. Is something going on between you two, Carolina?"

She shot me a look from the corner of her eye. "Just your run-of-the-mill marriage difficulties," she said.

"Good thing it's nothing more." He stood to refill his mug. "You can imagine how hard it is to spin a divorce between band members."

"Divorce?" Tony strode into the room. "Who's talking about divorce?" He glared at Carolina.

"No one," she said firmly, going over and taking his elbow. "Now let's talk about these new songs."

THE MORNING SEEMED to drag by, especially since I wasn't bringing my A-game to my barista duties. Although I remembered how to make the drinks, I felt like I was mentally preparing for someone to make another attempt on Carolina's life. Bo picked up the slack, and Bristol had also come in, so I was afforded a little space to think.

I'd advised Carolina not to eat or drink anything on the Crush Bus, just in case. She'd agreed to meet me at the nearby hot dog stand for lunch.

Summer emerged from behind a kiddie ride with two dogs on the leash...and my mouth gaped. One of the dogs looked alarmingly like a golden Labradoodle named Waffles who'd been in and out of both animal shelters and foster homes. Although Waffles looked adorable and she doubtless meant well, she was a constant whirlwind of destructive activity.

I pointed. "Is that—"

"Waffles," she nodded. She pulled the wayward dog tighter on the leash, effectively hiding her behind the crate. This was a good idea. Bo had commanded that Waffles was never to return to the cafe, due to the sheer havoc she'd caused last time. I couldn't imagine why Summer had brought her over today, given Bo's feelings for the ditzy dog.

She spoke in an urgent whisper. "Listen, I had to bring her because I really need to get this dog adopted, once and for all. Her latest foster parents turned her back over to the shelter today."

"Was she using the bathroom on the floor again?" I leaned in to pet Waffles because she really did seem to like me. She gave me a doggie smile and sat down as if she were any other well-trained dog. I knew better.

Summer glanced at Bo, who was busy with a customer. "Not this time. She was actually outside, free to roam. But that was the problem—she roamed too far and attacked the neighbor's chickens. Plus, she couldn't even hear the foster parents when they yelled for her, so she was missing meals while she was out on the run."

"Livin' large, were you?" I scratched behind Waffles' curly blond ear. "So what's your ultimate plan with her now?"

Summer leaned in. "I figured she couldn't cause any trouble if she stayed here in the crate, and maybe some fairgoers will fall for her. Anyone who shows interest needs to be asked if they have a fenced yard or if they're willing to put up an invisible fence. I think that would be the ideal environment for her. I mean, she can't be indoors due to accidents, but she can't be free to roam or she'll get herself—or maybe someone's chickens—killed."

I gave Summer a conspiratorial grin. "I understand completely. Waffles deserves a home, but it has to be a very *special* home."

"Exactly." Her long braid swung against her back as she crouched to open the crate. After walking both dogs in, she unleashed them.

Carolina strode over, wearing her straw hat and sunglasses. She held a plate with a hot dog on it and gave me a wave. She appeared to be alone, so I guessed the bodyguard had stayed behind at the bus. I was just about to introduce her to Summer when the dog crate burst open, sending Summer tumbling to the ground.

Of course, Waffles lunged out and took off running.

Bo, who hitherto had no idea that Summer brought the rogue dog in today, pointed. "Was that—"

"Waffles," Summer finished sadly, taking his hand as he helped her to her feet.

I was already running after the dog. "I'll get her," I shouted over my back. "Stay here, Bo!"

To my surprise, Carolina ditched her plate in a nearby trash can and bolted after me. "I'll help!" she called out.

Waffles' course was erratic, to say the least. She dodged several kiddie rides, deftly jumping over the tracks as if it were part of her daily fitness routine. She occasionally stopped to nuzzle into random children's hands as if searching for scraps of food. Then, in a burst of speed, she bolted toward the racetrack —where the horses were thundering by.

I lost sight of her momentarily and stopped to catch my breath, scanning the area with my hand up to block the midday sun. Just as Carolina caught up to me, I spotted the dog crawling under the bleachers. She must've pooped herself out. Carolina and I fanned out to approach her hiding spot. I gestured toward a kind-looking woman sitting near Waffles' makeshift dugout. She glanced down and realized what we were doing. Reaching in, she grabbed Waffles' collar and hung onto her until we got close.

Carolina and I converged on the woman, thanking her profusely. As she looked into Carolina's face, she got a little flustered. "Aren't you from that band?"

"No." Carolina point-blank lied. "Everyone tells me that, though."

I took Waffles' collar and she had the decency to drop her head, ashamed. That was the tough part—she knew when she'd run off the rails, but she just couldn't stop herself from going there.

As we weaved through the bleachers, I was more focused on Carolina's lie than on Waffles' impulsive behavior. Lying about her identity was probably a defense mechanism, one she'd developed over years of exhausting "sightings," but it still surprised me how easily she did it. I sighed. Maybe I was getting all judgey because I hadn't yet walked a mile in her designer leather boots.

I actually hoped I never did. Stardom wasn't for the faint of heart.

As we stepped onto the gravel next to the bleachers, Carolina stopped short and pointed. "It's Aidan," she breathed.

I followed her finger, and sure enough, the tall man was hustling toward us. He wore a jacket that was too heavy for the day and his hand was in his pocket. My defensive radar went up. He could easily be carrying a gun. Stepping in front of Carolina, I turned around and shouted. "Run!"

Aidan continued barreling my way. Waffles, confused as to why I'd stopped our delightful walk, started barking.

"Shh," I warned, hoping she wouldn't agitate Aidan more.

He slowed as he reached my side. Glancing all around, he said, "Where'd Carolina go? Is something wrong?"

I couldn't restrain myself. "Yeah, *you* are, dude. Why've you been following her all over the place?"

He looked—*really* looked—at me for the first time. I tried to read his dark eyes, but they were inscrutable. "I needed to talk to her about something."

"Well, stalking someone isn't the way to do that. Were you at my house yesterday...or the night before?" I demanded.

He gave a slow nod. "I was there yesterday—I went over and rang your doorbell, but no one was home." Without answering my question about the night before, he pulled his hand from his pocket.

Immediately, I shrank back, but there was nothing in it. Instead, he pointed at the stables. "I needed to tell her that I think her husband's involved in some shady stuff."

To my relief, Bo strode up behind Aidan and clamped a hand on his shoulder—the kind of unyielding grip that said he wasn't going anywhere.

"What's going on?" Bo asked.

Unfazed, Aidan repeated his story. "That guy Tony

Garten's involved in some stuff over at the stables. I've seen him and that older guy hanging out after hours. Last time I followed them, someone handed them some bags. I thought Carolina should know."

What older man was he talking about? Surely not Murphy Peters?

"I think you're a little too interested in Carolina," Bo said firmly. "Detective Hatcher has come to the fairgrounds to talk to you, so now we're going to walk back to the coffee stand so you can meet him." He looked at Waffles, then at me. "Are you okay with that dog?"

I gave a weary nod. "I think so. I'll head back to the booth as soon as I see where Carolina went to."

Bo nodded and led Aidan away. I rambled around aimlessly until he was out of sight, then I turned to walk Waffles toward the stables, because I'd noticed that Carolina took off in that direction. It was probably an excellent place to hide. Despite Bo's previous lecture, I figured I was safe enough heading over in the broad daylight to give her the all-clear.

Unable to stand completely upright with my fingers wrapped around Waffles' collar, I chided the impulsive canine. "You have to learn to control yourself," I said. As she turned her sad eyes up to me, I had to admit there was a real possibility that Waffles never *would* nail down the logistics of being an obedient dog. And I hoped she could find an owner who was actually okay with that.

16

I WALKED into the door of the near-empty first stable, surprised to find Carolina standing near Chancellor's stall. She was chatting with Murphy and a bald man I guessed might be a harness cart driver. But as I looked closer, I realized that while the man was trim and shorter, he was likely too old to race horses. He turned to look at me, and I felt some kind of weird electric charge as I stared into his eerily pale green eyes. It wasn't a charge of attraction—more of recognition—but I didn't understand *why*. I was quite certain I'd never seen the man before.

Carolina left off talking and made her way toward me. Waffles tugged at her collar, obviously interested in checking out the fascinating smells in the stables. "Hang on," I said, spotting a piece of twine on the wall. "Let me tie this on her."

Carolina came closer as Murphy continued talking to the other man. "Why's he hanging around the stables?" I asked quietly.

"Murphy? Oh, he has a share in Chancellor, so he tries to

keep up with his races," she said. "What happened with Aidan?"

I explained that Aidan must've been following Tony over to the stables, where he'd watched him and some older man pick up some kind of delivery that was bagged up. "I'm not sure what the story is with Tony, but Bo has taken Aidan straight over to meet up with Detective Hatcher," I said. "So that situation is under control. I should let Mattie know."

Carolina nodded. "Good grief. I love Lewisburg, but this visit has been awful. I can't wait to fly out. Gage is meeting me at the airport," she added.

I wrapped the twine around my hand, hoping Waffles would take the hint and sit down, instead of acting like she was ready to spring at any moment. "But what'll happen to Carolina Crush?"

She hedged. "It seems impossible now, but we need to keep going. Of course, I'll have to find a new backup singer, and once Tony finds out about Gage, I'll have to talk him into staying on."

"Why?" I asked. "He might be on drugs, or at the very least he's blowing all his money on gambling. Why would you want someone like that in the band?"

She flashed me a serious look. "Tony's got such a unique sound on the dulcimer. We can't afford to lose him, so I'll make sure we don't." She placed a hand on my shoulder. "Macy, I had to ask myself a long time ago how far I was willing to go to become a household name. Trust me, begging Tony to stay is child's play compared to the kind of effort I've given to become the face of Carolina Crush."

Summer burst through the stable doors, a blue leash in hand. She came directly over and clipped it on Waffles' collar. "I'm sorry it took me so long to find you, Macy," she said, shooting Waffles a frustrated look. "I guess this girl's going to have to stay in the shelter and hope for someone to find her there. No more field trips."

Waffles whined and sat down at my feet. A groom walked in with Chancellor, saying the horse had won the race. Murphy pumped his fist in the air, and the man standing with him smiled.

But then I noticed who was walking—or rather, crouching—directly behind the beautiful stallion. Boaz Hatfield, my brother. And his gun was in his hands.

"Get *down*," I hissed at Summer and Carolina. Summer did as I said, falling into a pile of straw. But Carolina stood stock still, giving me a confused look. "What?"

"Stay right where you are," Bo said, pointing his gun at Murphy and the bald man.

Before I could register what was happening, Carolina bolted out the door. Waffles yanked on her leash, ready to give chase.

Bo turned for a split-second, just in time to see Carolina running away. "Get her!" he shouted to me.

I didn't have time to ask myself why Bo wanted me to stop my old friend. Handing Waffles' leash to Summer, I instructed her to stay put and keep the dog on top of her. As I raced toward the door, I noticed the groom was reaching for a pistol in the back of his pants.

"Bo!" I shouted, frantic that he recognize the danger he was in. I was about to turn back to help when I saw three men in DEA vests rushing toward the stables. "In there!" I pointed, knowing Bo would want me to catch up to Carolina before we lost her.

As I caught sight of Carolina's red polo shirt bobbing between the horses that were leaving the track, a couple of shots rang out in the stables. "Keep running," I told myself, picking up my pace. "Do what he asked you to do."

While I wasn't the best long-distance runner, I could sprint when the occasion demanded, as it did now. I started closing in on her. Carolina tore her straw hat from her head and dropped it to the ground, probably because it was obscuring her view as she ran. When she rounded the corner of the bleachers, I was just about to grab her when she smiled back at me and put on a burst of speed, her long legs propelling her faster than I could hope to go.

She tore across the open grassy area, straight for a narrow pathway between two tents. I was sure to lose her if I didn't speed up, and I was already getting worn out.

But before she could dart into the opening, a group of teenage girls that had been loitering nearby—possibly smoking—gave shouts of recognition. They began to form a semi-circle that blocked the path between tents, so Carolina was forced to slow down so she didn't crash right into them.

It was my one chance. I sped up, running straight into Carolina and tackling her to the ground.

The teens gave screeches of fury. "Hey, I got that all on video!" one shouted, trying to pull me off Carolina.

I was starting to fear I'd be pulled limb from limb. "Call 9-1-1," I commanded. "She's in trouble with the police." I wasn't sure about that, but I was guessing there was a reason she ran from the stables.

The girls glanced at each other, then started shaking their heads. One girl who was wearing short shorts and a leather halter top stepped forward. She flicked a lit cigarette toward my feet. I assumed she was the ringleader. "Lady, you all kinds of crazy. We ain't doing nothing for you. Now you let Miss Carolina go."

I leaned more heavily on Carolina, who was trying to wriggle out from under me. "No, I'm telling you—"

"Hello, ladies," a deep voice said. I twisted around to see the six foot five inch figure of Titan McCoy looming behind me. Another man stood beside him. Titan flashed his badge. "We're with the FBI, and my friend here is going to chat with you while I contain this situation."

The girls groaned. I rolled off Carolina, more than happy to get *out* of the situation. As Titan clicked handcuffs on her and helped her to her feet, she practically snarled at me—a far cry from the best friend of my youth.

But I didn't have time to try to understand why Carolina was so irate. "Titan, can you leave your guy here and go back to the stables with me? I left Bo there and—"

Titan shook his head. "Bo's okay. Our people are there with him."

"But I thought this was a DEA case?" I asked.

"It is, but both teams are working together for a big fish, so to speak. We came for the man who owns Chancellor—and who's been facilitating the drug drops on the fairgrounds."

Was he talking about Murphy? Carolina had said he had a share in Chancellor. Or was it Tony? Was he a much bigger player than I'd thought?

Before I was able to ask Titan about the man they were hunting—and whether or not they had managed to get him—Bo and Summer slowly walked our way with Waffles panting along behind them on the leash. Bo's arm was draped around Summer's shoulders, and he leaned heavily on her, his mouth set in a grim line.

I ran over to him. "What happened? Are you okay?"

Bo gave me a wan smile. "I'm fine, sis."

Summer gave him a dubious look. "Well, not entirely fine." Turning back to me, she explained, "He got shot, but he was wearing a vest under his shirt. It knocked him flat—Macy, I was so scared. I almost crawled over to him, but I remembered what you'd told me about staying down and hiding under Waffles, so that's what I did." She reached down to pet the curly dog's head. "Waffles seemed as shell-shocked as I was, so thankfully she didn't take off running. Just then, those DEA men came in and took down the groom who'd been shooting."

We approached Titan, who gave Bo a brotherly clap on the shoulder. He didn't make any small talk. "Did you get him?"

Bo's jaw hardened. "No. When the groom shot at me, he ran out the side door. By the time my men searched for him, he'd disappeared. We figure he had an escape vehicle waiting."

Titan pounded his large fist into his palm. "We were so close this time."

"It's no one's fault that it took us so long to figure out what was really going on. There was a lot of subterfuge." He stepped over toward Carolina, who was standing with the other agent. "You used my sister," he accused, obviously gathering strength.

There was no trace of the formerly flirtatious singer as Carolina sneered at Bo. "I thought you were supposed to be so tough. You didn't even guess what was going on right under your nose."

Really? She just said that to *my brother* who had done nothing but tried to protect her this entire time? I strode over and got right up in her pretty face. "I don't know what you've done, *friend*, but I'll tell you one thing—you're no one's hero. My brother actually *is*, however, and many times over. And all those girls that worship you"—I gestured to the nervous teens who were still loitering to watch events unfold—"They're going to see who you really are."

I was contemplating spitting on one of Carolina's pretentiously blingy cowgirl boots when Titan motioned for the agent to haul her off.

Waffles gave a melancholy whine. Bo glanced down at her. "We need to move out of the hot sun and find some water for the dog," he said.

"Let's head back to our stand so we can fix iced drinks for us, too," I suggested. I looked at Titan, noting how his thick brown hair had grown out and was curling up at the ends. "Care to join us?"

I figured he'd beg off and say he had to travel back with his partner, but he nodded. "I'd like that."

17

Bristol greeted us with warm smiles—especially Titan, who had done her family an exceptionally good turn last December. He asked about her talented younger brother, Ethan. Bristol happily shared that Ethan's kidney transplant had gone very well, and that he loved working from home as a computer whiz for the FBI.

Bo apologized for leaving Bristol alone at the booth so abruptly. His men had been watching the stables, and they'd determined that they had to move immediately to make the bust. Bo was closest to the stables, so he wound up leading the charge. Titan and his crew were already on the fairgrounds, so they were close behind.

After filling a water bowl for Waffles, who slurped up nearly as much as Coal would, we opened the crate. For once, the doodle was happy to do exactly as we wanted, stepping directly into the shaded crate and placing her tired head on her golden paws.

"What a dog," Summer remarked.

I pulled out folding chairs and made Bo sit down. Titan

and Summer arranged themselves next to him, and I walked over to help Bristol make iced lattes for all of us.

As I handed Titan his, the sunlight lit up the gold in his maple brown eyes. "Thanks, Macy." The curls in his hair were so out of sync with his agent persona. Although the man's sheer size and presence made him completely intimidating, I had the strongest feeling that he had a soft heart under his FBI veneer.

He took a sip. "This is great." He stretched his long legs out, and for a second I thought he was going to collapse the small canvas chair. He gave an annoyed grunt. "I can't believe we didn't get him."

"You mean Murphy?" I asked. "Was he the kingpin who was running drugs?"

Bo shook his head. "No, sis. We're talking about Leo Moreau."

As a wave of comprehension engulfed me, I nearly choked on my coffee. "Wait—no—that was Leo in the stables? The bald man?" I recalled that unaccountable recognition I'd felt when I looked into those icy green eyes.

Bo nodded. "That was him. Hadn't I showed you a picture of him before?"

"You hadn't." It was rather inexplicable that some strange, deep part of me recognized the sheer evil of the man in the stable, sight unseen. Leo Moreau had been involved in so many underhanded dealings and murders over the years—I knew Bo hadn't even told me the half of it. Sometimes our gut reactions were right.

But then again, I had welcomed Carolina into my home, and now it seemed she was somehow involved with the drug operation. I struggled to understand how all the pieces fit together, especially given the obvious attempts on Carolina's life. Hadn't she been the victim?

I took another quick sip of latte. "I'm trying to make sense of things. So Murphy was involved in the drug smuggling? And Tony? But what about Carolina?" I asked.

Bo gingerly leaned back in his chair. "Murphy was Tony's dealer—and we'll probably find that he was a dealer for other stars, too. That was his first profession, before he became a manager, so it was easy to maintain his old connections with Moreau to keep his big-name clients supplied."

"So Tony was on drugs," I murmured. "But what about Carolina? How was she involved?"

Titan glanced at Bo. "When Detective Hatcher brought Aidan in today, he admitted that he'd followed Carolina to your house on Monday night and parked on the street outside. Later that night, he heard voices at one of your side windows, so he crept closer."

"Aidan Conley was a stalker though, let's just get that straight," Bo interjected. "He's no innocent here. He needed to know where Carolina was at all times. He said he was waiting for the perfect opportunity to have her sign his Carolina Crush T-shirt, but we know that's just a cover story. From the moment she came back to town, he tracked her every move."

"Poor Mattie," I said quietly.

Summer nodded, taking a sip of coffee.

"She's going to be okay," Bo said. "I'm going to have a counselor friend talk her through things. Just because Aidan's in jail for a little while doesn't mean he's going to be perfectly normal when he gets out."

Titan returned to the subject at hand. "Stalker or no stalker, Aidan helped us out tremendously by sharing what he overheard that night. A man—he was fairly certain it was Tony—was talking to Carolina. He told her he'd dealt with her problem. Unsure what Tony meant, Aidan followed him around the next day and saw him meeting up with Moreau's drug goons in the stables. He assumed Tony meant he'd gotten drugs for her, so he got worried that she might be an addict."

Bo picked up the story. "After the detective talked to Aidan today, he reported Tony's involvement to Titan. Since the FBI had already arrived on the fairgrounds, they found Tony on the bus and questioned him. Given that Gage had just announced that he and Carolina were flying back to Nashville together, Tony was more than happy to turn on Carolina and share about her master plan."

"Master plan?" I was bewildered. "What do you mean?"

Titan leaned in and actually placed a steadying hand on my knee. "I'm sorry, but your friend is a schemer, Macy."

"She's a murderer," Bo said shortly.

"What?" I said, in complete disbelief. "You mean she killed Reya?"

"Not directly," Bo said. "See, Carolina doesn't use drugs—she uses *people*. She convinced Tony to get rid of Reya for her."

"But why would she want to do that? Was she jealous that Reya was trying to grab the limelight? Did she think she was going to replace her?"

Titan shook his head. "She wasn't worried about that. What she *did* worry about was that Reya had approached Tony, demanding answers for the extension cord with the severed ground pin. See, she'd checked that cord before the show and she knew it was fine. But since she stood toward the back when she sang—close to Tony—she'd put two and two together and realized that when the lights went down and she'd heard Tony moving around, he must have crept up and cut the cord in the dark."

"That's what they were arguing about when you saw them from the Ferris wheel," Bo explained. "But Reya didn't grasp the big picture. Tony hadn't cut that cord in hopes of killing Carolina. He'd cut it *on Carolina's orders*."

Summer whistled. "You're saying she wanted to kill herself in front of all her fans? That seems extreme."

Titan jumped in. "Oh, no—she had no intentions of killing herself. That's why she wore the thick-soled boots. She'd read that rubber soles had once protected another singer who'd been shocked on stage. It was the same thing when she ingested the Digoxin. She only ate enough to make her sick, not to kill herself."

I sat in silence, completely dumbfounded. Why had my friend taken such outlandish risks?

Titan continued. "We did some digging and discovered that Carolina Crush wasn't as successful as you'd think. Their profits were quickly getting eaten up by a serious lawsuit—Carolina's old roommate from Nashville claimed she'd written the lyrics to 'Not Forgotten,' and it looked like she was going to win that suit."

Things were starting to make sense. "Plus, Tony had frittered away all his band earnings on gambling and drugs, which placed them in a precarious financial position," I added.

Titan nodded. "Exactly. Carolina saw a way to increase public sympathy for her while skyrocketing the band's publicity. She'd convinced Tony that she was doing everything for the two of them, but she was gearing up to throw him under the bus. She knew exactly what he'd used for a murder weapon—a wooden mallet from the strongman game where you pound the base and try to hit the bell. He told us that he'd hidden it until the police search was over, then he planned to clean it up and sneak it back to the fairgrounds later."

I was hit with another epiphany. "I'll bet she was using Gage, too, letting him think she was going to start a new life with him."

"Oh, yeah. I doubt she really cared about him, either," Bo said. "In reality, I'm guessing the only person she loves is herself. She probably planned on striking out on her own to become a soloist, taking all that public sympathy with her."

"A narcissist, through and through," Titan said. He looked at my knee, as if he wanted to put his hand on it again. "Macy, I'm sorry."

I felt like a fool for trusting Carolina, for asking her into my house, for believing all her stupid lies about everything. I leaned over and put my head in my hands.

Summer reached over to rub my back. "You couldn't have known she was such a...a *user*," Summer said. "If I'd have known she was such a jerk, I would've punched her for you."

I raised my teary eyes to Summer's serious brown gaze and laughed. "So much for your peaceful Mennonite upbringing," I said.

She grinned and reluctantly stood to her feet. "Guys, I have to get these dogs back to the shelter. I'm afraid it's time to launch another Waffles adoption campaign."

"Good luck," Bo said wryly.

"I'll stop by your place later, if you don't mind," she said, hooking the dogs to their leashes. "I plan to make supper for you and Macy since you've both had an awful day."

"Sure, that'd be great." Bo struggled to his feet, obviously in some pain. "I'd better reconvene with my team, too." He glanced over. "Charity's here now and Jimmy should show up soon. Do you mind closing up for me later, Macy?"

"I'm happy to do it," I said.

Once everyone had cleared out, Titan gave me a long look. "You doing okay?"

I was about to give a glib answer, but I couldn't. Liars like Carolina and Jake made me even more determined to be as honest as possible with others...and even with myself. "It's hard," I said. "Maybe I was blind to who Carolina really was— not just now, but all those years ago, too. Bo once heard her talking bad on Auntie A, and now that I think about it, maybe a lot of what I believed about Mattie's bullying was simply exaggerated secondhand stories that Carolina fed me. Not that Mattie was ever nice, but maybe she wasn't the monster Carolina made her out to be."

"It's a classic narcissist move—she made you doubt others' motivations so you'd trust her more. Did she ever try to come between you and Bo? It seems like you and your brother have always been tight."

"Come to think of it, she used to say Bo was irritating because he'd try to look out for us. Even on this visit, she was calling him a skinny ginger...until she saw him in person. Then she was so surprised, she started flirting with him."

Titan chuckled.

I was still musing. "And do you know what she was talking about, just before everything went down at the stable? She said she'd decided a long time ago just how far she was willing to go to become a household name. Apparently that included making risky attempts on her own life for publicity purposes and ordering for her backup singer to be killed because she was asking too many questions."

"It's all about her." Titan looked off into the distance as if his thoughts had flown elsewhere.

He seemed to know a lot about narcissists, and I wondered if he'd been close to one himself at some point. Just another mystery about this man I really wanted to get to know better. I heaved a burdened sigh before I could stop myself.

"Hey, would you want to take a few minutes and do bumper cars?" Titan asked suddenly. "They bring back such good memories. I'm warning you, though—I'm an excellent driver."

I laughed. "You don't say. Well, I'm not so shabby myself.

Yes, I'll take you up on your bumper car challenge." I jumped to my feet.

We walked over and after a few minutes in line, we chose our cars. Titan tried to pick the longest one, but he still had major issues trying to fold his legs into the tiny vehicle. I was chuckling so hard that by the time I hit the gas, I ran straight into the kid's cart in front of me. The poor child, probably no older than seven, shot me a frustrated look and gunned it as hard as his cart would allow.

Titan had already made a loop and he came back around, grinning as he smashed into my bumper. I shouted and hit the gas, making a wide loop to take him out, but when I came in to hit him, he managed to dodge me. We spent the rest of our time acting like two overgrown children and hunting each other down.

After crawling out of our cars at the end of the ride, I boasted, "I hit you more than you hit me." I felt grubby and victorious.

"That's because I let you," Titan said.

I gave him a playful shove. His unusual eyes met mine. "Now, don't you forget who you're messing with," he joked.

There was no way I was going to do that. In fact, I was only a little *too* aware of what a powerful, yet equally kind man Titan was.

"You're not awful for a McCoy," I said flippantly.

"And you're tolerable—for a Hatfield," he said.

After we parted ways by the hot dog stand, I caught sight of myself in a mirror by a display of sunglasses and realized I needed to wipe the goofy look off my face. But I knew why it was there. Despite the unbelievable discovery that my old friend had lied to and used everyone in her path, Titan had made this day memorable in another way, and I was grateful for him.

18

A LIGHT THUD hit my head and a small round beanbag fell to the ground. I turned to see a woman running toward me. She wrung her hands together, apologizing as she approached. "I'm so sorry! My daughter lost her grip on that beanbag and it flew out in the other direction! Are you okay?"

I rubbed at my head, which felt perfectly normal. "I'm just fine." I grabbed the beanbag and handed it to her. Taking the longer route back to the Barks & Beans booth so I'd dodge the children's game area, I ducked into a stand that was selling scarves and flags. I immediately felt someone's eyes on me, so I turned, expecting to find the salesperson glowering.

It took a moment, but my eyes finally lighted on a woman who stood in the corner of the tent. She wore a scarf draped around her in such a way that it covered her face. I gave her a smile, waving to reassure her that I wasn't about to steal anything. Her eyes darted toward mine again...and I realized she wasn't a woman at all.

Those piercing green eyes belonged to the man I'd just met —the man who wanted my brother dead. Leo Moreau.

Knowing better than to attack the hardened criminal, I backed up and dashed away, weaving through the vendor tents. As I ran, I took out my phone and called Titan, hoping he was still around.

He was about to leave, but he assured me he was on his way and he'd get his agents on it, too. Back at our Barks & Beans booth, I waited anxiously for what seemed hours. In reality, only forty minutes had passed when Titan walked over to let me know they'd canvassed the entire fairground, and Leo had not been located.

I was still reeling. "I can't believe he was right there, staring right at me."

Titan was serious. "I'm going to call Bo."

After touching base with my brother, Titan reported that Bo's DEA agent friends would also be keeping an eye out for Leo. In the meantime, Bo had asked Titan to escort me home, since Leo had definitely seemed aware of who I was in the scarf booth.

Titan walked me to my car, where I sat and waited until he pulled up behind me in his black SUV. He followed me home. I got out of the car while he was finding a parking space on the street.

Vera was working in her front yard and she called out for me. "Macy! How are you? Listen, am I right in thinking your friend owns that tan Lexus?" She pointed a gloved finger to a car parked on the curb in front of her house.

I glanced over at it. "She was renting a car, but I'm not sure if that was the one."

As Titan stepped from his SUV, Vera's eyes widened. I tried to see him for the first time through her perspective. He was an exceptionally tall, built man with dark hair and an intense, dead-level gaze. He wore a loose shirt that likely covered a gun. His tough-looking, somewhat dirty boots said he knew how to hold his own outdoors.

But then he offered her a polite smile, and all I could see was a gentleman who genuinely cared about others. Extending a long hand, he introduced himself. "Hello, Ma'am, I'm Titan McCoy."

"And I'm Vera Cox," she said. I could tell by the way she kept staring at him that she'd forgotten all about the Lexus.

I cleared my throat. "Uh, was there something you were worried about with the car?" I glanced at Titan, unsure how much I was allowed to share about Carolina at this point. "My friend might not be back for a while, but I can find out if it's hers."

Vera gave an earnest bob of her head. "Oh, I'm pretty sure it is. I saw her get out of it last night. I just wondered if someone could move it before tomorrow when the book club ladies come over." She dropped her head a bit. "That's actually my parking space."

I immediately felt bad. "Oh, sure, I'll figure out a way to do that," I promised. I didn't want to be a nuisance to my neighbors in any way.

"Thank you, hon," she said, reluctantly tearing her gaze from Titan. "I'd better get back to work while the weather's nice."

"Okay, I'll talk to you later," I said.

Titan lingered by my fence. "I'll grab the plate number and find out where she rented the car," he said. "I can tell them to pick it up since Carolina won't be able to return it."

I opened the gate. "Did you want to come in for a second and say hi to Coal?"

He smiled. "I wish I could, but I need to get over to the station—they'll be questioning Murphy soon. But please tell your doggie hello for me."

Feeling a pang of sadness, I asked, "What's going to happen to Carolina?"

"She won't be singing in the band anymore, let's put it that way. Both she and Tony conspired in Reya's murder, even though Tony was the one who actually bludgeoned her to death."

I gave a gloomy nod. Carolina had so much going for her—sure, Carolina Crush wasn't where it needed to be financially, but it certainly wasn't defunct yet. They could've rallied by writing more hit songs, but instead, Carolina had sacrificed all her integrity on the altar of fame. She had been fearless, but in all the wrong ways.

Pulling the gate shut, I said goodbye to Titan and walked toward the house. My phone rang and I picked up without checking the caller ID.

"Hey, sugar."

The moment I heard the southern drawl on the other end, I hit the speaker button and ran back to the fence, gesturing wildly to get Titan's attention. He turned and walked back to me. We both watched my phone in silence, listening to Anne Louise Moreau on the other end.

"Listen, I know my husband's been kicking up trouble over there in the stables, but you might as well call off the manhunt for him. He's got people everywhere, and I heard he's nearly made it out of the state now. But, Macy honey, I want you to pass some information along to your brother. You tell him he needs to investigate the Carson deal in Ecuador. Thank you kindly." She hung up.

Titan and I stared at each other. "How'd she get my number this time?" I asked.

He frowned. "Anne Louise tends to get what she wants."

"And now she wants Bo to check on something in Ecuador? What's that all about?"

Titan looked frustrated. "I don't know. I'll call and talk with him. But Anne Louise is up to something. From the hints she's dropping, she might be gearing up to go against her husband."

"Doesn't he have people protecting him all the time?"

"Oh, sure. But I'm thinking she won't hit him out in the open. She's the type who would know exactly how to tear his operation apart from the inside. As we've seen in the past, she has some loyal henchmen."

I shivered. I didn't want my brother aiding Anne Louise at all, but Leo had wrecked Bo's old life in many ways. Bo probably wouldn't be able to resist checking into the Carson deal.

"This has *not* been the best day." I shoved my phone into my jeans. Looking up at Titan, I hastily revised my statement. "Except for the bumper cars, of course."

His warm eyes met my own. "I agree."

LATE SATURDAY AFTERNOON, Vera and I sat on my back porch, sipping glasses of mint-sprigged lemonade. Coal had stretched out along the top step, soaking in the sunlight. I was enjoying the fact that my fair-working days were over for this year.

Of course, things hadn't slowed down much at the cafe. Bo was already brainstorming a first-anniversary celebration for Barks & Beans in September, but I knew that in the meantime, he'd also bitten on Anne Louise's suggestion that he look into the Carson deal. It was apparent to everyone that his attention was split—especially to Summer. To my dismay, he seemed to have left her a little high and dry.

Vera interrupted my thoughts. "He's handsome," she mused.

I glanced over at her, taking in a deep smell of someone's freshly-cut grass. "Who?"

"That Titan, hon. And he seemed...I can't explain it...but he seemed connected to you somehow."

I blushed and took a big gulp of cold lemonade.

"Now listen," Vera continued. "I promised I'd tell you all about your Aunt Athaleen, and I think now's as good a time as any. You should know what a strong woman she was." She patted my hand. "Years ago, my husband Russ got to where he refused to let me see the bank account and he wouldn't even give me a straight answer when I asked him how much money I could spend on groceries. On top of that, my mother's emerald ring went missing from my jewelry box. I got so frustrated, one day I just up and asked him if he'd taken my ring and hocked it. Of course, he swore he didn't."

She shook her head. "I was sick of his lies. I lived up the street from your aunt then—in that green house on the corner. She'd always been so good to talk to me at church. One day, I told her all about Russ' behavior, and she offered to help me get to the bottom of things." She chuckled. "I'll tell you what—there was no one who could formulate a plan like your great aunt. Long story short, we wound up following Russ to an abandoned house just outside town. A fancy Cadillac drove up, and a couple of men wearing dark hoods got out and headed into the house to meet Russ. By the time Russ headed back for his car, he had a black eye."

"What had happened to him?" I asked.

"We weren't sure, but we figured he owed someone money and the black eye was a warning. We kept an eye out for that Cadillac...and one day, it came back to town. I was over at the library at the time, but your aunt caught sight of it and trailed it. And guess where it went?" She gave a little clap of her hands, unable to control her excitement. "To the mayor's house!"

I looked closer at her soft-featured face, trying to picture both her and Auntie A as the Nancy Drews of their day. It was difficult to imagine.

Vera continued. "Your aunt listened outside a window, and she overheard the mayor and these out-of-towners talking about some kind of shakedown operation they were running that involved scamming hard-working local men out of their savings. Men like Russ. We told your aunt's old boyfriend, Detective Mercer Priestly, about it."

Auntie A had an old boyfriend in town? I wondered how Uncle Clive had felt about that, but then again, she'd never given us any illusions that she and Uncle Clive were very compatible. He'd died in his fifties, before she adopted us, and even after that, she'd never had much good to say about him.

Vera beamed. "Because of your aunt's help, our family changed for the better. Once Detective Priestly busted the mayor and his gang wide open, Russ was freed of those debts. He turned into a different husband and father—so caring and attentive." She sipped her lemonade. "I never got to properly repay your aunt, but now that I've moved back, I want you to know my gratefulness extends to both of you Hatfields. Anytime you need anything, you just ask."

Coal stood and stretched, probably anxious to get out of the sun. I set my lemonade down and ran a hand along his back. It was comforting to know that Bo and I weren't the only ones who had experienced the unwavering selflessness of Auntie A.

"I surely will," I said.

I'D JUST CHANGED for bed and padded downstairs to make a cup of chamomile tea when I got a call. It was the police station, so I picked up, figuring Detective Hatcher had some questions for me.

"Hi," Carolina said.

I nearly dropped the phone. "Uh...hi."

"You're my one phone call," she said, her voice falsely cheery. "Murphy already got me a lawyer. I wanted to tell you I'm sorry, Macy. I let you down."

"You let everyone down," I said grimly.

Her voice dropped. "I know."

Sun-spun memories of childhood flitted through my head, but I shoved them down. "Did you want to tell me something?"

She rallied. "I did. Listen, I still have some money socked away in stocks. I want you to transfer those to Claude's name. My baby brother doesn't deserve to have to completely fend for himself, and I know my parents won't do anything to support him at his age. I'll have my lawyer get all the information to you."

I choked up a little. "I'll do that," I promised.

"And Macy," she added, her voice wavering, "Don't ever take your brother for granted."

I gave Coal's big head a pat, fully aware that I wouldn't have met him or even moved back into this house if Bo hadn't thought up the Barks & Beans Cafe.

"I never will," I said.

You can now preorder Heather Day Gilbert's next Barks & Beans Cafe cozy mystery,

SPILLED MILK

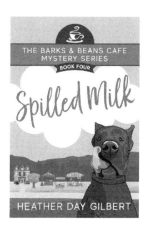

Welcome to the Barks & Beans Cafe, a quaint place where folks pet shelter dogs while enjoying a cup of java...and where murder sometimes pays a visit.

The fall flea market has arrived in Macy's small mountain town, and she's taking a day off work to check out the local wares. As she and her Great Dane, Coal, wander through the booths, Macy's more than a little taken aback to discover that her enigmatic tattooed barista, Kylie, is selling antique weapons at the event.

She's even more shocked when Coal sniffs out a dead body...and the man appears to have been struck down by one of Kylie's swords.

As rumors begin to circulate, the Barks & Beans Cafe also takes a hit. Customers are reluctant to order their mochas from a murderess. Macy stands by her employee, but even she believes there's a whole lot more to Kylie's history than the woman lets on. To make matters worse, Macy's brother Bo is out of the country, leaving the cafe's future in her hands.

And then her ex-husband Jake shows up, begging to make amends.

With the past rearing its ugly head, Macy has to ignore Jake's distractions, appease the angst of her nervous customers, and convince Kylie to trust her, all before an elusive killer strikes again.

Join siblings Macy and Bo Hatfield as they sniff out crimes in their hometown…with plenty of dogs along for the ride! The Barks & Beans Cafe cozy mystery series features a small town, an amateur sleuth, and no swearing or graphic scenes. Find all the books at heatherdaygilbert.com!

ALSO BY HEATHER DAY GILBERT

The Barks & Beans Cafe cozy mystery series in order:

Book 1: No Filter

Book 2: Iced Over

Book 3: Fair Trade

Book 4: Spilled Milk

Be sure to sign up now for Heather's newsletter at heatherdaygilbert.com for updates, special deals, & giveaways!

And if you enjoyed this book, please be sure to leave a review at online book retailers and tell your friends!

Thank you!

Printed in Great Britain
by Amazon

51659066R00092